'I made a bad choice.'

Sasha refused to think about the implications of Grady's revelation. That he might want to come back for her. It wasn't possible. And even if he did it wasn't going to happen. She was done with risking her heart.

Grady placed his hands on her shoulders. 'We all make mistakes, Sasha. But please stop thinking your baby's mother is bad. You are so special. She'll never want for love or kindness. You have those in bucketloads. When you touch your tummy your eyes go all misty with it. She's a very lucky little girl.'

Talk about knocking her for six. Never would she have imagined Grady saying something so heart-warming, so caring.

'Thank you,' was the best she could manage around the tears clogging her throat. She reached up to place her hand on his cheek. 'I needed to hear that.'

His eyes locked with hers. So much emotion streamed out at her. Too many emotions to read.

'If you did then I'm glad I told you.'

Her stomach hurt from clenching. Her head throbbed from holding in the tears. And her heart ached—because in a different world, at a different time, Grady would have been the perfect man for her.

Dear Reader

Golden Bay is one of New Zealand's gems. There's only one road in, but it's well worth the effort to go there. I've spent a few summer holidays staying at one of the beaches there, enjoying the fishing, swimming and just relaxing. I also have family living there, and I attended a wonderful wedding on their lawn which gave me ideas leading to these stories.

Sasha and Grady, Jessica and Jackson—all have family connections and history from when they were teenagers. But people have to leave the bay area if they want to attend university, and not everyone comes back. Of course I had to bring these four back. I hope you enjoy their ensuing relationships and how they find love again.

Cheers!

Sue MacKay

PS I'd love to hear from you at
sue.mackay56@yahoo.com
or visit me on www.suemackay.co.nz

The second story in Sue MacKay's
***Doctors to Daddies* duet**

THE MIDWIFE'S SON

**is also available this month
from Mills & Boon® Medical Romance™**

A FATHER
FOR HER BABY

BY
SUE MacKAY

First published in Great Britain 2014
by Mills & Boon, an imprint of Harlequin (UK) Limited,
Large Print edition 2014
Eton House, 18-24 Paradise Road,
Richmond, Surrey, TW9 1SR

© 2014 Sue MacKay

ISBN: 978-0-263-23916-4

Harlequin (UK) Limited's policy is to use papers that are natural, renewable and recyclable products and made from wood grown in sustainable forests. The logging and manufacturing processes conform to the legal environmental regulations of the country of origin.

Printed and bound in Great Britain
by CPI Antony Rowe, Chippenham, Wiltshire

With a background of working in medical laboratories and a love of the romance genre, it is no surprise that **Sue MacKay** writes Mills & Boon® Medical Romance™ stories. An avid reader all her life, she wrote her first story at age eight—about a prince, of course. She lives with her own hero in the beautiful Marlborough Sounds, at the top of New Zealand's South Island, where she indulges her passions for the outdoors, the sea and cycling.

Recent titles by Sue MacKay:

FROM DUTY TO DADDY
THE GIFT OF A CHILD
YOU, ME AND A FAMILY
CHRISTMAS WITH DR DELICIOUS
EVERY BOY'S DREAM DAD
THE DANGERS OF DATING YOUR BOSS
SURGEON IN A WEDDING DRESS
RETURN OF THE MAVERICK
PLAYBOY DOCTOR TO DOTING DAD
THEIR MARRIAGE MIRACLE

These books are also available in eBook format from www.millsandboon.co.uk

Dedication

Thanks very much to Kate Vida for her medical help. Any mistakes are mine. And to Deidre and Angela, because I can.

Praise for Sue MacKay:

'An emotional drama full of powerful feelings and emotions. An immensely satisfying read on all counts—a wonderfully human story which will leave the reader moved. I look forward to reading more books by this author in the future.'
—*Contemporary Romance Reviews* on
THE GIFT OF A CHILD

'The first book in this duet, THE GIFT OF A CHILD by Sue MacKay, is a deeply emotional, heart-rending story that will make you smile and make you cry. I truly recommend it—and don't miss the second book: the story about Max.'
—*HarlequinJunkie*

'What a great book. I loved it. I did not want it to end. This is one book not to miss.'
—*GoodReads* on
THE GIFT OF A CHILD

CHAPTER ONE

AS SASHA WILSON reached the first sharp hairpin bend on her descent from the top of Takaka Hill into Golden Bay she eased off the accelerator, moving even slower than her previous snail's pace.

A shudder rolled through her chilled body, nothing to do with her friend's entreaties for her to move back to the city where her biggest mistake ever lived but all about the treacherous road conditions. While there was frost on her heart, it was the black ice at every corner and coating most of the road that required her undivided attention right now. As it had done for the more than five hours she'd been driving home from Christchurch. Where her headlights swept the grass and tree-covered banks, blinding-white frozen water glittered back at her.

'Winter sucks,' she growled, and swiped the

back of her glove-covered hand across the condensation on the windscreen. 'If only it wasn't so important to be back for work in the morning, I could've waited until the weather cleared.' Then her voice softened and her hand briefly touched the bump over her stomach. 'At least you're tucked up nice and warm in there, Flipper. And safe from that selfish man who accidentally fathered you. The man who wanted me to terminate you.'

Gasp. 'Wash my mouth out.' Flipper wouldn't pick up on her thoughts, would she? Because no matter her own opinion of the man who would remain nameless, she wasn't ever going to visit that on her daughter.

Gripping the steering-wheel, she continued her diatribe. 'It's like someone threw a switch on my life. Winter's always been about chasing the best snow and hurtling down ski slopes, and going to those amazing après-ski parties to rub shoulders with some of the best skiers in the world.'

Not any more. Her skis were in a cupboard at the back of her parents' shed. Her fancy outfits were folded away in cases filling the wardrobes in the tiny cottage she now lived in on the edge of the family orchard.

'We don't even like the cold, do we, Flipper?'

The baby kicked none too gently.

'You're quite the swimmer, aren't you?' Sasha smiled as she sucked in a breath. 'The inside of my tummy must be bruised purple from your feet.' Pregnancy was amazing. Every day seemed different. She already loved her little girl. Completely and utterly. Fiercely. She'd protect her with her life.

On the radio a song finished and the announcer piped up in his false cheery voice, 'Coming up to eleven-thirty on the clock, folks. I hope each and every one of you is tucked up warm and safe by now.'

'I wish. Big time.' Sasha flicked a glove-covered finger in the direction of her radio. 'You obviously haven't listened to your station's weather forecast, buster. It's been blowing a blizzard up and down New Zealand for most of the day and some of us are struggling to get home in the resulting chaos.'

Successfully negotiating a tight bend, she let

relief spread through her. 'One down.' The relief evaporated instantly. 'Plenty more to go.' If only she was pulling up outside her house now. She was so over this trip.

A new, cheerful song filled the interior of the car as Sasha leaned forward to peer through the windscreen. 'It's hideous out there, Flipper.' Not even the possums were out partaking in their nightly forage for dinner. She shivered and hunched her neck down into the warmth of her leather jacket.

Her mouth stretched wide as she yawned. She was tired beyond tired. The long drive down to Christchurch on Thursday, the pre-wedding celebrations, in which, as bridesmaid, she had an active role, and then the wedding yesterday—she'd been on the go non-stop for three days. And then today's endless drive from hell. If only keeping her job wasn't so important that she had to get home. But it funded her decision to return to the one place on earth where she felt safe, where there were people she could trust, where her family lived. Where Mum needed her.

Golden Bay with its small township of Takaka

had become her bolt-hole, the place where she could lick her wounds and harden her heart, the district she wanted to settle down in and raise her daughter. Earlier she'd briefly considered calling one of the doctors she worked for and explaining that she'd be a day late getting back, but they'd been adamant she had to prove her reliability if she wanted to get a permanent position at the medical centre. No days off for anything except illness, she had been told on more than one occasion. Her reputation from her long past high-school days just wouldn't go away. Small communities had a lot to answer for. But that was why she was here, that sense of a blanket being wrapped around her and keeping her safe and warm had also drawn her in.

Another yawn lifted her shoulders, filled her lungs. Rubbing her eyes, she spoke loudly in an attempt to banish the loneliness suddenly enveloping her. 'Hey, Flipper, ready to tuck up under our quilt? I know I am.' She really was nuts, talking to the baby like this. But it made a change from yakking to herself all the time. And it was good to talk to her baby even before she was born, right? Who cared? She'd do it anyway. There'd be people who said it was the right thing to do, and others who'd say she was bonkers.

'Unfortunately the cottage will be cold enough to freeze the boll—' *Oops, mind your language in front of the baby.* 'It'd be great if your grandma has gone down to light the fire for us. But somehow I doubt it. She doesn't trust the safest of fireboxes.' Mum had always been overly cautious. Mum. Sasha's mouth drooped into the antithesis of a smile while her eyes misted.

'What has Mum ever done to deserve the disease slowly wrecking her life, taking over her body?' she asked around the lump clogging her throat. Her beautiful mother, who'd always been there for her and her brother, refusing to accept the disease taking hold in her body would never let go.

Sniff, sniff. Life could be so damned unfair. Sasha's hands tightened on the steering-wheel as she leaned forward, all the better to see, but it didn't make the slightest difference. This final stretch of road seemed interminable.

'What the heck?' Red lights blinked from the

edge of the road ahead, right on the bend of the next hairpin. Random. Definitely out of place. Suddenly her heart beat a rapid rhythm.

'I don't like the look of this.' Her bed beckoned even harder. Swallowing a yawn and resisting the urge to slam on the brakes, she gently slowed to a stop right beside the rear end of an upside-down truck poking up from the bank it'd gone over. 'Bad parking.' But hardly surprising, given the hazardous road conditions. And why she hadn't relaxed at all despite getting close to home.

Sasha carefully turned her vehicle so the head-lights shone onto the wrecked truck, with its black tyres pointing up into the night. Down-right eerie. A shiver ran down her vertebrae. For a brief moment she wanted to drive on home to that cold bed and not face what might be waiting in that buckled cab. Not because of her need to be home safe but because all the years working in emergency departments hadn't dulled the fear she might fail someone who desperately needed her help. Neither did her nursing experience make seeing people suffering any easier to deal with. She felt for them, had cried tears for them.

'Get on with it,' she said. 'You can do the emotional stuff later when everyone in that vehicle's safe.' Because the truck hadn't driven itself off the road, and the glowing headlights suggested it hadn't happened long ago.

None of that stopped her muttering, 'Please, please, be empty.' Her churning stomach mocked her. 'Okay, then be safe, not seriously injured.'

Tugging her woollen hat down around her ears and pulling at the zipper on her jacket to try and close the gap caused by her baby bulge, she hauled in a lungful of warm air before elbowing the door open and gingerly stepping down onto the frozen road. Instantly her feet skidded sideways and she grabbed for the door, hung on as she righted herself. This wouldn't be a picnic, and these days, with Flipper on board, she had to be extra, extra careful.

Her cheeks instantly tightened from the cold, while her unease increased. Initially the night seemed silent but now the cracking sounds of hardening ice became apparent. Or was that the truck shifting?

'Nice one, Sasha. Scare yourself, why don't

you? Move your butt and stop overthinking the situation.'

Collecting her medical kit and the heavy-duty torch she always carried, she gingerly crunched over to the edge of the bank, and gasped. In the half-light the Golden Bay Freight Lines logo on the side of the truck was distorted but readable. Sam and Lucy Donovan's truck. 'Sam, is that you? It's Sasha.'

'Help me.'

'Sam, are you on your own?' Please, she muttered. Talk about needing a lot of favours in one night.

'No, the missus is with me. She's hurt bad, Sasha.'

Damn, damn, triple damn. The Donovans were the greatest neighbours her parents had ever had, always there for them, there for her too nowadays whenever she needed help with Mum's orchard. Which she didn't. Not because she was stubborn or anything. Of course not.

Sam hadn't finished with the bad news. 'I can't move my legs.'

'I hear you.' First she needed to get more help.

Fast. Her heart sank. What were the chances there'd be cellphone coverage? But she couldn't do this on her own. 'Has anyone driven past since you went off the road?'

'Not that I heard.' Sam's voice cracked. 'Hurry, Sasha. Lucy's bleeding from the head.'

Things were looking up. Not. Her heart squeezed for the middle-aged couple stuck in that cab. 'Sam, you'll have to hang in there while I get the rescue crews on the way out.' She swallowed her growing worry. Like worrying helped anybody. Thinking logically was the only way to go.

Tugging her phone free of a pocket, she touched icons. No coverage. Sasha glared upward at the stars blinking out of the now-clear sky. 'Thanks very much. Can't someone up there make it a little bit easier to save my friends?'

Crunch, crack. She jerked. Had the truck moved? 'Sam?'

'Sounds like another car coming.'

Yellow light slashed across the white landscape, swept over her. Relief poured through her tense muscles. She glanced upwards again. 'Okay, I take it back. Looks like there was already a plan in action.'

A car pulled up beside her. The driver's window opened a crack. 'What's going on? You need a hand, lady?' a voice she didn't know asked.

I'm not standing out here for the hell of it. The air in front of her face turned misty as she sighed. *Give the guy a break. At least he stopped.* 'A truck's gone over the bank with two people inside. We need emergency services urgently.' The risk of hypothermia was enough to want to rush everything, to drag Sam and Lucy out regardless of injuries. Which was so not how to go about rescuing them. 'I'm not getting reception. Can you call it in from further down the hill? Or stop at the first house you see? Tell them Sasha Wilson is here.'

'On my way.' The car was already moving away, thankfully cautiously.

But as she watched the lights fade in the distance that loneliness grabbed at her again. Until help arrived, Sam and Lucy's fate depended on her.

'Your problem is? You're a nurse. Not a bad

one either. Get on with doing something practical. Sam will be getting desperate.'

With all the ice about the place she wasn't in for an easy time getting down to the truck, something that never normally fazed her. But with Flipper to consider there'd be no leaping over the embankment like a surefooted goat. 'Hey, I can do careful,' she whispered. 'This is one time where I have to go slow and steady.' Now, there was a first. Her lips pressed hard together, the skin of her cheeks tight.

Maybe if she'd gone slow and steady with that greaseball back in Christchurch she'd still be up to leaping over edges without a care in the world. Might not have a baby under her belt. 'Sorry, Flipper. I'm not trying to wish you away, sweetheart.'

Wrong time to be thinking about this, with the Donovans waiting for her. Taking a steadying breath, she let her medical pack slide down the bank. Then, with her torch gripped tight in one hand, she sat down on her bottom and shuffled and slipped down, too.

'Hey, there.' She mustered a cheery tone as she reached the driver's door.

Sam blinked in the light from her torch. 'Am I glad to see you.'

'How secure do you think the truck is?'

'I haven't felt it move at all. From the sound when we hit I think we're jammed against rocks.'

Some good news. At least they weren't about to plummet down to where the road twisted across the hillside directly beneath.

'Sasha, I'm real worried about Lucy.'

The fear in Sam's voice had her squatting down by the shattered window to shine the torch inside. Blood had splattered over most of the interior. Lucy hung upside down, half in, half out of her seat belt, a huge gash across the side of her head.

'She hasn't said a word the whole time.' Sam's voice trembled. 'What if—?' he choked.

'Hold that thought, Sam.' Darn, but she hated it when friends were hurting. Placing her free hand on Sam's shoulder, she tried for a reassuring squeeze. 'I'll check Lucy over. But what about you? Where are you hurting?' At least he was upright, though what injuries he'd sustained when the truck had rolled didn't bear thinking about.

'To hell with me. Look after Lucy, will you?'

'Okay. But keep talking to me.' The way his voice faded in and out didn't bode well. 'Tell me where you hurt. Did you bang your head?' He had to have, surely? 'Are you bleeding anywhere? Stuff like that.' Talking might keep him focused and make the minutes tick by a little faster than if he just sat watching and worrying over his wife. Really? That was the theory but theory often sucked. 'Shine my torch so I can see what I'm doing.'

Hand over hand she grabbed at the edge of the truck's grille and made her way to the other side. Not easy clambering over frozen rocks with a bump the size of a basketball under her jacket. Flipper must've got the seriousness of the situation because she'd gone nice and quiet with those feet. Automatically rubbing her tummy, Sasha muttered, 'Thanks, sweetheart. Mummy owes you.'

Reaching through where the window used to be, she felt carefully for Lucy's throat and the carotid. 'There you go. Lucy's got a pulse. She's alive, Sam.'

One big sniff. 'Thank you, lass. Can you get her down from that seat belt? I don't like her hanging like that. Can't be doing her any good.'

'We're going to have to wait for the rescue guys. I could do more damage than good if I cut her free.' Tilting her wrist to see her watch, Sasha counted Lucy's pulse. Slightly low but not too bad, considering. 'You haven't told me about your injuries yet, Sam.'

Carefully feeling Lucy's head, neck, and arms for injuries, she tried to work out how long would it take for the rescue crowd to get here. How long since that car had driven away? Had the driver got that this was an emergency? Swallow hard. Toughen up. It would be at least forty-five minutes before anyone showed up. Make that an hour by the time everyone'd been phoned. Then there were the road conditions to contend with.

Focusing on diverting Sam's attention—and hers—she said, 'You and Lucy were coming home late.'

'Been to tea with the kids in Nelson.' He went quiet.

A glance showed his eyes droop shut. 'Sam.'

He blinked. 'Roads are real bad.'

'Very dicey.' It wasn't the first time she'd driven this road in the aftermath of a winter storm, and it probably wouldn't be the last. Unless she changed her mind about staying in Golden Bay like Tina wanted. Now her friend was a happily married woman she seemed to think she had the right to fix Sasha's life. Worse, the guy Tina had thought would solve all her present problems had been nice—in a wet blanket kind of way. Tina was probably making up for the fact she'd introduced the greaseball to her in the first place.

'Sorry, Tina, but which bit of no more men for me didn't you get?'

'Who's Tina? Is someone else here?'

'Talking to myself. A bad habit I really should get over.'

Taking a thick cotton pad from her kit, Sasha taped it over Lucy's head wound. Hopefully that would slow the blood loss. She kept prattling on about anything and everything in an attempt to keep Sam with her. Having him slip into unconsciousness would make it harder for the rescue crew to remove him.

Glancing at her watch, she stifled a groan of despair. Twelve-twenty. The rescue crews couldn't be too far away now. Could they? What if the road was worse between here and Takaka? Don't even go there. She knew those men, had gone to school with some of them, now worked with others. They would come through. It might take some effort and time but they'd be here as soon as it was humanly possible.

'S-Sasha, h-how's Lucy?' Sam's teeth clacked together as shivers rattled him.

Sasha winced. A couple of thermal blankets would be very welcome right about now for her patients. Her own toes were numb, her fingers much the same since she'd removed her gloves to attend to Lucy, and she wasn't stuck, unable to move. At least Flipper would be warm. She answered, 'Breathing normally and the bleeding's stopped.'

After what felt like a lifetime flashing lights cut through the dark night. Relief slipped under her skin. 'The ambulance's here. Now we'll see some action.'

The first voice she heard was Mike's, one of the GPs she worked for at the Golden Bay Medical and Wellbeing Centre. 'You down there, Sasha?'

She stood upright, grabbing the doorframe for balance. 'Yep, and I've got Lucy and Sam with me.'

Before she'd finished telling him, Mike had joined her. Rebecca, one of the ambulance volunteers, was right behind him.

Mike asked, 'What've we got?'

'Sam's legs are caught under the steering-wheel. Lucy's entangled upside down in her seat belt.' Sasha quickly filled them in on the scant medical details. Above them a tow truck pulled up, quickly followed by another heavy four-wheel-drive vehicle. Then the fire truck laden with men equipped with cutting gear and rescue equipment arrived. 'I love it when the cavalry turns up.'

Mike grinned. 'Guess it does feel like that. You want to wait in the warmth of the ambulance? Thaw out a bit before we send one of these two up to you?'

For once she didn't mind being set aside so others could get on with the job. She wasn't in a position to take the weight of either Lucy or Sam as they were freed and lifted onto stretchers. The strain might affect her baby in some way and that was not going to happen. 'On my way.' Though it wouldn't be as easy going up the bank as it had been coming down.

Mike read her mind. 'There's a rope to haul yourself back up to the top, as you're more of a small whale than a goat these days.'

She swiped at his arm before taking the end of rope he held out to her. 'Thanks, Doc.'

'Is that Sam's truck? Is he hurt badly? Anyone with him?' The questions were fired at her before she'd even got her feet back on the road.

Doing her slip-slide ballet manoeuvre and with a lot of men reaching for her, she managed to stand upright and steady. 'Lucy's unconscious and Sam's fading in and out.' Sasha glanced around at the mostly familiar faces, relief that they were here warming her chilled blood.

Then she froze. Like the air in her lungs had turned to ice crystals. The heat left her veins.

Her eyes felt as though they were popping out of their sockets. *Tell me I'm hallucinating.* Her head spun, making her dizzy. Her mouth tasted odd as her tongue did a lap. *Can't be him.* Her numb fingers hurt as she gripped someone's arm to stay upright. *Not now. Not here.*

But, of course, she wasn't imaging anything. That would've meant something going in her favour for a change. Grady O'Neil was for real. Eleven years older and more world-weary but definitely Grady. No mistaking that angular jaw, those full lips that were nearly always smiling—except not right at this moment—and… Her shoulders rose, dropped back in place. He hadn't been smiling the last time she'd seen him either. When he'd told her he didn't love her any more he'd had the decency to keep at bay that wicked smile that made her knees melt. The first man to hurt her. But he didn't have that on his own any more. There'd been others. She so didn't do well with picking men.

The urge to run overwhelmed her. Her left foot came off the ground as she began turning in the direction of her vehicle. *Sliding on the ice and falling down hard on your butt would be such a good look. And could harm Flipper.* Deal with this. Now. Breathe in, one, two, three. Breathe out. 'Grady.' She dipped her head. 'It's been a while.'

A while? How's that for a joke? Why wasn't he laughing? A while. Far too long. Huh? No. She meant not nearly long enough. Didn't she? Oh, yeah, definitely not long enough. Yet here he stood, a few feet from her, as big and strong and virile as ever. And that was with layers of thick warm clothes covering that body she apparently still remembered too well.

You shouldn't be remembering a thing about that amazing year. You're long over him and the hurt he caused. True? Absolutely.

She fought the need to revisit Grady and everything he'd meant to her, instead aimed for calm and friendly, as though his unexpected appearance didn't matter at all. 'What are you doing here?' Big fail. Her voice rose as though a hand gripped her throat. Memories from those wonderful carefree days she'd stashed away in a mental box some place in the back of her head were sneaking out and waving like flags in a breeze, threatening to swamp her.

Swallowing hard, she focused on now, not the past. Why had Grady turned up? Golden Bay was her territory. Not his. He'd only come for summer holidays and that had been years ago. He'd be visiting. But who? Not her, for sure. Her tummy sucked in on itself, setting Flipper off on a lap of her swimming pool, nudging Sasha every few seconds, underlining how unimportant Grady was in the scheme of things.

Sasha dug deeper than she'd ever done before for every bit of willpower she could muster to hold off rubbing her extended belly. She would not draw those all-seeing blue eyes to her pregnant state. That was hers alone to cope with. She certainly didn't need Grady asking about her baby.

His smile seemed genuine, though wary. Which it damn well ought to be. 'Hi, Sash. This is a surprise. I didn't expect to run into you while I was here.'

Sash. That certainly set free a load of hot memories. Her nipples tightened, her thighs clenched.

Grady still drawled her name out like he was tasting it, enjoying it.

He couldn't be. He'd lost any right to those sensations the day he'd told her he didn't love her enough to spend the rest of his life with her. Yet he was checking her out. Her pulse sped up as that steady gaze trawled over her, starting with her face and tracking slowly down her chin, her throat, over the swell of her breasts under the thickness of her jacket, on down to Flipper. As his gaze dropped further the breath she'd been hanging onto trickled over her lips. He hadn't noticed the six-month bulge. Guess the thick jersey and heavy jacket she wore made her look larger than normal anyway.

Now his gaze had reached her legs—forever legs, he used to call them. Another memory leaped out of the box. Grady's strong hands gently rubbing sunscreen from her toes to the tops of her thighs. Slam. The lid shut firmly.

Then Grady stepped right up to her and enveloped her in those strong arms she would not remember. Her head bumped against the chest she'd never found the likeness of again. And out of nowhere came the need to lay her cheek against him and tuck her hands around his waist. Even to tug that shirt free and slide her hands over his skin.

No, Sasha, you can't. Are you that stupid you've forgotten his parting words? That memory never went into the box. That one you kept out in the open as a warning never to make the same mistake.

Except she had got it wrong again. Had learned nothing in the years since Grady. She jerked backwards. Too quickly for him to let go of her, so that her baby bump shoved forward, right into his solar plexus.

His head snapped up, those startled eyes registering shock. He pulled away from her fast, as though he'd walked into an electric fence. In the shadows and flashing lights from the emergency vehicles she saw a multitude of questions spinning her way. He pushed his hands deep into his jacket pockets, forced his chest out and splayed his legs slightly. Such a Grady stance. The don't-mess-with-me posture even while his face showed how much he wanted to ask her about that bump.

Tough. Her baby had nothing to do with him. He'd want to know who the father was, no doubt wondering if it was someone he knew from way back when they had been part of a whole crowd of teens at the beach. He could guess all night long, he'd never get it right.

He looked away, looked back at her. Tugged one hand free and rammed his fingers through his thick hair. Stumped.

She blinked as her throat clamped shut on the delayed shock charging up her body, opening that box of memories again, wider than ever. *I remember you very well, Grady O'Neil. Too well. I remember—too many things I'd prefer not to.* The air trickled out of her lungs. Those memories were capable of melting all the black ice on the Takaka Hill road.

Why had she never considered this moment might happen? Because Takaka had been their playground only when they'd been teenagers knocking around together. Knocking around? That was one way of describing what had gone on between them. They'd been inseparable. Totally in love with the intensity of teenagers overdosed on hormones. She'd stupidly thought they'd be together for ever.

So wrong about Grady. So wrong about the greaseball she'd walked away from four months ago. She really needed a 'how to' book on establishing perfectly balanced relationships with the opposite sex.

She closed her eyes. Opened them. Nothing had changed. Grady still stood in front of her, questions blinking out, begging for answers. No way, sunshine. Not telling you. Swallowing the lump in her throat, she croaked, 'I didn't realise you knew Mike.'

'I met him two days ago when I dropped by the medical centre. He and Roz invited me to have dinner with them tonight, which is where I was when this call came in.'

Jonty called from the open back doors of the ambulance, 'How do we get these stretchers out of here?'

Saved by the fireman. Sasha hurried to clamber

inside the wide vehicle and unlock the stretchers from the wheels they wouldn't be using tonight.

'Ta.' Jonty grinned. Then pulled a grim face. 'We're bringing Lucy up first so you and Grady can do what you have to with her in the warmth of the ambulance.'

I have to work with Grady? Her skin broke out in goose-bumps, even as she gathered her strength around her like a mantle. 'Sure.' She pressed her lips together and started getting out equipment they'd need. She'd work with the devil if it meant helping Sam and Lucy.

The devil might be easier to get on with.

Blinking back a sudden rush of tears, she tried to concentrate on the job. Damn her tear ducts. They'd taken on a life of their own since she'd become pregnant.

The ambulance rocked as Grady clambered up the step. Did he have to suck up all the air? Surreptitiously she studied him, saw the pinching at the corners of his delectable mouth. Absurdly she wanted to reach out and touch him, run her finger over those lips and say, Hello, how've you been? *Great idea, Sasha. Not.*

'Sash, can you move back a bit so I can get inside?' His vivid cerulean eyes locked onto her and the bottom fell out of her stomach. That memory box lifted its lid again as she looked deeper into those eyes that used to twinkle at her while sending her hormones into a dance, eyes that had undressed her, grown slumberous with desire. Eyes that had turned the colour of thunderclouds as he'd told her they were over. Eyes that now held nothing but a simple request.

So he was playing the friends card. She'd do that too. Cool, casual. Aloof even, but friendly.

Flipper chose that moment to kick hard, making her gasp. Sinking down onto the stretcher frame, she rubbed her side. Felt another nudge from her girl. This baby had an attitude problem. Reminding her mum exactly what her new life was all about—her daughter.

CHAPTER TWO

'SASHA WILSON, I'VE never forgotten you.'

He sucked cold air through clenched teeth. Unfortunately his mind remained fixed on Sasha.

'Not for lack of trying, believe me. You've hung around in my skull, annoying the hell out of me, reminding me continually of what I destroyed. My one chance of extreme happiness blown out of the water because I couldn't figure a way to make the future work well for both of us at the same time as looking after Mum and my sisters.'

What had he done to deserve this turn of events? Opening up old wounds had never been on his agenda. Especially Sasha's hurts. Coming to Takaka had been such a foolish idea, but he'd thought spending four weeks here would be safe. That he'd visit, get his house sorted and on the market then leave, without Sasha factoring into his plans—because she wouldn't be here.

When Mike had mentioned her name earlier he'd struggled to absorb the shock and warmth that had hit him. But it seemed no preparation could lessen the slam-dunk feeling he'd got when he'd actually seen her. His ability to think straight had vamoosed. He'd been sorely tempted to hold her, kiss her, devour her. The struggle to keep himself together while he'd given her that friendly hug had caused knots in his shoulders and neck muscles.

And then her pregnant belly. That had really put him in his place. He didn't belong here. Certainly not with Sasha. But, then, that was why he'd come, to get shot of his house and move on with his life. Once and for all.

Sash hadn't lived here for years, or so he'd been told. If anyone had told him she was working at the local medical centre, however temporarily, he'd have said they needed to see a shrink. Golden Bay was far too small for a personality the size of hers. Always had been. *They'd* never planned on living here any time in their future. The future he'd deliberately destroyed to set her free.

He didn't want to think about that baby she carried. But how could he not? His heart slammed his ribs. A little bit of him had died right then. Sasha was pregnant. With another man's baby. Yeah, well, the point being? Pregnancy usually involved a man and he hadn't been around for a very long time. Bile soured the back of his throat. She'd got on with her life like he'd told her to, proving how final his words had been.

He'd spoken them but had he understood the true depth of what he'd told her? Hurting her had been unavoidable if he was to make her get on with her life, unhindered by his problems with his family that had suddenly tied him to Nelson and stopped him going away to med school. He'd spent hours trying to come up with a way to break off with her without causing her distress and pain, hoping to leave the door open for later. Of course there'd been no answer other than to say it straight out. Go, get on with your life, leave me to mine. It had hurt him as much as her, but she hadn't seen that.

Now Sasha had a family of her own. Without him. His loss. His big loss.

Was that what had brought her back here? Family? The baby's maternal grandparents lived here. The slower-paced, outdoors-orientated lifestyle was perfect for a young child. Sasha had lots of friends here who were probably starting families round about now. Who had she settled down with? Someone local that he knew? Or an outsider who'd fallen under Sasha's spell? Like he had the very first time he'd set eyes on her as she'd rowed her dinghy into the beach and tossed the anchor at his feet. He'd been young and horny and in lust. Which had quickly turned to young and horny and in love.

Where was her man anyway? Grady scowled. *He* wouldn't have let her out alone at this hour, driving in these horrendous conditions. Yeah, but this was Sash. The woman who never listened to anyone's advice. The girl with enough confidence for a whole team of downhill skiers. That had been one of her attractions. That and her smarts, and her enthusiasm for just about everything— except spiders and mashed spuds.

Never in a month of dry Sundays had he expected to feel so disorientated when he saw her.

He'd honestly believed he'd be cool, calm and casual. He'd had an hour to prepare. He'd been sitting at the same table as Mike, listening as the guy had rung around the emergency volunteers, getting them on the road to help Sasha with a road accident.

The only word that had registered in his brain had been 'Sasha'. Immediately excitement had rolled through him. He was going to see her. For eleven years he'd stayed away, wondering how she fared, if she'd forgiven him, and could they be friends again—and now all he could think was what he'd missed out on. His gut roiled. Sasha, his one true love. Out of reach for ever. And no one to blame except himself.

How could I have been so stupid to think I'd get over her if I tried really hard? Talk about impossible.

Pain bounded around his chest. His head spun so fast it hurt. His gut had crunched down hard, feeling like it held a solid ball of concrete. So much he wanted to know, yet he couldn't ask her a thing.

'Ask what?' came the sharp tone of the woman

he wanted to pretend wasn't within touching distance.

Inside the ambulance he ducked to avoid smashing his head on the overhead cupboards. 'Nothing,' he muttered, because he truly couldn't think what to say. Most things that came to mind would be incendiary. Certainly not conducive to good working relations.

A cupboard door slid shut with a bang. 'What area of medicine did you specialise in?'

So she knew he'd finally trained as a doctor. She must've thought of him occasionally, then. Was that good? Or bad? He told her, 'I chose general practice. I like the community aspect best.'

'I get that.' Sasha surprised him with a smile. A very brief flicker but he'd take it. It melted some of the forced wariness that had settled on his heart the moment he'd seen her head popping up from behind that bank where the truck had crashed. The chill had been about him, not her. A hopeless attempt to shut down any leftover feelings he had for this beautiful, feisty woman.

She'd been a girl-slash-woman when he'd fallen in love with her. Seventeen going on thirty. Unafraid of anything, whether it had been taking her dad's plane up for a spin, galloping her horse at breakneck speed along the beach, or diving for scallops out in the bay. She had always got her own way by sheer willpower. People had either gone with her or stepped aside to watch with envy her latest escapade. Watching her now, she seemed very much in control.

Voices reached them, and then thankfully men appeared at the entrance to the interior of the ambulance. Jonty was telling them, 'Go easy with that stretcher, guys. Lucy doesn't need any more knocks.'

Sasha took the top end and guided the stretcher onto its frame, before deftly clicking all the locks in place. Lucy wasn't going anywhere she shouldn't.

Grady moved closer, looking their patient over, fighting to ignore Sasha's presence as her arm rubbed against his when they both leaned over the stretcher. Heat spilled through him. Heat that woke up parts of his body best left asleep right now. Heat he did not need around Sash. *Focus on Lucy.* Head wound, right arm at an odd angle, suggesting a fracture, laboured breathing. Sliding a hand under Lucy's torn blouse, he carefully felt her ribs. No problems there. One point in her favour.

'The GCS was nine when I first checked Lucy and it hasn't changed,' Sasha informed him. 'She came round twice very briefly earlier and asked about Sam, before losing consciousness again.'

The Glasgow Coma Index. Borderline severe. Not a good sign. Grady's fingers worked along Lucy's hairline then over her head. 'I'm guessing she hit the dashboard when the truck flipped.'

'The wound above her temple was still bleeding moderately when I reached her.'

He gently lifted the padding at one corner. 'It's stopped now.'

'One thing to be thankful for.' Sasha's tone was perfectly reasonable, normal. Totally unaffected by his presence.

Guess she'd long got over him. Which, considering her pregnancy, should be mighty obvious even to his sluggish brain. He must've done a good job of telling her to get on with her life without him in it because the results were very clear. Sash was going to become a mother in a few months' time. She hadn't done that on her own.

The green-eyed monster lifted its head, roared inside his skull. Who was the lucky bastard? Did he treat her well? Did she love him? Completely and utterly? Passionately? Of course she did. That was the only way Sash did anything. Grady wiped his hands down his jeans, removing a sudden coating of sweat. 'We need to splint Lucy's arm.'

He'd spoken more brusquely than he'd intended and received a perfectly arched eyebrow kind of glare for his trouble. 'Sure.'

It was as easy as that for Sash. Except her fingers had a slight tremble as she handed him the splint. Interesting. And confusing. Talk about mixed messages. Not only were those fingers trembling, they were covered in rings. Was one of them a wedding ring? The silver one on her wedding ring finger had a tiny butterfly etched into the metal. Not a likely wedding ring, even for Sasha.

They worked quickly and efficiently, routine

emergency care that neither of them had any difficulty with. Grady asked in as nonchalant a voice as he could manage, 'Where have you been working? Before Takaka?' Sasha had been planning on starting her training only weeks after the last time they'd been together. They'd finished high school and had been enjoying their last summer holidays before hitting the adult world.

'In the emergency department at Christchurch Hospital for a year.' She gently lowered Lucy's arm by her side. 'Now I'm the community nurse around here while the centre's usual nurse is on maternity leave.'

'Must be something in the water,' Grady muttered.

'Here I'd been thinking it was all to do with loving relationships.' Suddenly her tone could have slayed rampaging bulls.

A quick glance showed the anger spitting out at him from those beautiful emerald eyes. Anger and something else he couldn't make out. Hurt? Disappointment? It had come and gone so fast he didn't have time to work out exactly what that emotion had been.

'Sash, I'm sorry. I didn't mean to sound flippant.' Once he'd have been able to say anything to her and get away with it. That had been before bust-up day. Eleven birthdays and Christmases ago. A doctor's degree ago. Two broken relationships ago. Relationships he hadn't cared enough about to make work.

'My name is Sasha.' Words as cold as that ice outside fell into the silence.

Not to me you're not. His heart cracked wide open at her rebuff. He hadn't set out to be overly friendly by using his pet name for her. But he'd *always* called her Sash. He hadn't learned not to. All these years he'd thought about Sash, not Sasha. That was everyone else's name for her. She used to protest at anyone calling her Sash— except him. Seemed he'd been relegated to the slush heap. His shrug was deliberate and heavy. 'Sasha.'

The door opened and cold air hit them as Mike and the guys hoisted the second stretcher on board with Mr Donovon strapped down tight.

Their patient roused himself enough to croak out, 'How's Lucy?'

'She's stable, Sam.' Sasha held the older guy's hand for a moment, spoke in a very caring way, nothing like she'd talked to him. 'I'm glad you're out of that truck.'

'You and me both, lass.'

Mike nudged his way between Grady and Sasha. 'Let's take a look at you, Sam, before we get on our way.'

'Are you driving over to Nelson?' Sasha's eyes widened. 'I've just come over the hill and it's not good. Took me a lot longer than normal.'

'No choice. The rescue helicopter flew to Wellington on an emergency run four hours ago and has been grounded after a wind gust flicked it sideways, causing damage to a rotor,' Mike explained. 'Jonty has offered to drive while Rebecca and I keep an eye on these two.'

Rebecca poked her head through from the front, where she'd been having no luck in her attempts to raise the Nelson ED on the radio. 'I don't have a lot of confidence driving on ice, whereas Jonty's had plenty of practice.'

'You want me to come along?' Grady asked

Mike. 'I'm happy to help.' Though it was getting crowded in here.

Mike shook his head as he cut down through the centre of Sam's trouser leg. 'No point in all of us missing out on a night's sleep. Rebecca and I can handle this. Grady, you hitch a ride back with Sasha. She lives on her parents' property, close by your house.' Mike really didn't have a clue about anything.

He saw Sash stiffen for a brief moment. Then she returned to helping Mike, for all the world completely unperturbed by the other doctor's suggestion. Mike's idea made perfect sense. She lived very close to his house. He used to be able to get to Sasha's in under a minute on his motorbike if the road was clear. Bloody lucky he'd never come off on that tight corner by the Wilsons' gate. 'Okay with you, Sasha?' he drawled.

Why did his mind play these games to annoy her when really all he wanted was a bit of peace for the rest of his stay here? He must quit giving the woman a hard time. She hadn't asked for him to barge back into her life. 'I can go back with the fire truck if you'd prefer.'

Her mouth tightened, her eyes darkened, and she tugged those small shoulders back hard, automatically pushing that baby bump further out between them. She wouldn't back down from what she'd been asked to do. But she glared at him as she said, 'Might as well come with me. I warn you I'm not in a hurry. Too much ice to drive like I'm handling a racing car.'

Now, that was something new. Sash had always driven like she had to win. 'Works for me.'

'Let's go.' Sasha was blunt. 'I'm more than ready to be home tucked up in bed for what's left of the night.'

Air whooshed out of his lungs. Sash and bed. The memories he'd been trying to deny for the last thirty minutes reared up bright and dazzling. Sash—gregarious, generous, sexy, funny. A full-on, crazy, risk-taking kind of girl. An exciting, adventurous lover whose kisses had always left him breathless. And wanting more of her. What he wouldn't do for one of those now.

Huh? Man, he had a problem, and he was about to hitch a ride with her. He watched her carefully lower to the ground, holding onto the safety rail in case her feet went from under her. So unlike the Sash he knew. But he wanted, needed, to get to know this version.

Mike tapped him on the shoulder. 'Sorry about dragging you up here, but that's Golden Bay for us medicos. The isolation means no one can ever totally relax.'

'No problem,' he answered mechanically, his eyes still fixed on Sash as she moved away awkwardly, taking each step extra-carefully. Her back ramrod straight, her head high. He knew her chin would be jutting forward, her mouth tight.

Exactly like that last time he'd seen her. On the sand at Pohara Beach below Dad's house, now his house. She'd turned to walk away from him, the summer wind flattening her burnished gold curls and sandblasting her arms. Her long legs, forever legs, showcased by barely-there shorts, had eaten up the ground as she'd put distance between them.

Those green eyes, big in her fine-featured face, had been fixed on something in the distance at the far end of the beach. Only minutes before they'd been filled with love for him. Love that had rapidly turned to disbelief, and pain, as he'd spewed out his sorry attempt to make her go away so she could have the future she'd already mapped out long before they'd got together. The only kind of future that would suit Sasha. Certainly nothing like the one he'd suddenly faced, brought about by Dad's death.

If he had a dollar for every time he'd wished his words back over the intervening years he could have retired already. But there'd be no undoing what his mouth had spilled that day. His deliberate attempt to send her on her way had been highly successful. Though he'd been thankful it was done, there'd been a part of him that had wished she'd fought him, made him accept there was no letting go of what bound them together, that theirs was a love that would see them through anything and everything.

Now he had to sit in a vehicle with her for as long as it took to get home. He would not spend the trip remembering her fingers playing over his skin in moments of wild passion. He would not recall how she'd call on her cell phone in the middle of the night and talk dirty till he lost control. Or how she'd climb on the back of his motorbike, slide her arms around his waist and hang on, laughing at the wind in her face. Not. Not. Not.

His heart squeezed painfully. He'd missed Sash so much that even if he could, he didn't want to go away again without talking to her. Could they bury the elephant between them? These weeks might be his only opportunity. He could put the time to good use and put the real Sasha up against the one in his memory. That might prove interesting. Maybe the biggest disappointment of his life. But then he might finally be able to move on.

'You going or what?' Mike asked.

Grady shook his head, concentrated on the here and now. 'On my way.'

He hadn't even got the car door shut before Sash turned the key in the ignition. She mightn't intend driving fast but she wasn't wasting time hanging around. Glancing his way, she kept her face inscrutable. 'Ready?'

'Yes.' Shrugging back into the corner, he couldn't stop his gaze wandering over her. His breathing stuttered. She'd grown even more beautiful than he remembered her to be. Her pearly whites were now straight and orderly. The braces she'd hated wearing had done a fantastic job, though he missed the gap between the two front teeth. That had been kind of cute. Sasha's curls had grown into a long, burnished gold ponytail held firmly in place with a purple clip thing. She still stared directly at everything, everyone. Including him.

And there—in those eyes—he finally recognised something from way back. Those eyes held the same all-seeing, missing-nothing gleam, and they were focused entirely on him. Looking for what?

Then she blinked, turned her head and began backing the vehicle onto the road, before concentrating on taking them down the hill. Her hands were firm on the steering-wheel, her body tilted forward as she peered out the windscreen. She was in control. Nothing new there. But she wasn't fighting the situation, instead using the gears to go with the conditions outside.

Grady relaxed further back into his seat, clicked his seat belt in place. The vehicle was in capable hands. Unless fate had some ugly plans for them he'd soon be back at his house, warm and comfortable again. And hopefully getting some sleep. Something he seriously doubted was likely to happen.

The only sound was the purr of the engine and the intermittent flick, flick of the wipers. Sasha had never liked silence. But she wasn't doing anything about filling this one. Grady's mouth twitched.

Ironic but he wanted to hear noise, her voice, words, anything but this quietness that smothered him.

Her gloved right hand lifted from the steering-wheel and did the gentlest of sweeps across her belly.

His gut squeezed tight. He wanted to place his hand on top of hers, to feel whatever she felt. To be a part of this scene, not an observer. Her gesture had been instinctive, a mother-to-baby touch. Sash was obviously comfortable with being an expectant mum. It suited her.

From what he could see in the dull light from the instrument panel her face had softened, the glint in her eyes quietened, and that chin didn't point forward. Yes, she was at ease with her situation, if not with him.

The tightening in his gut increased. He wanted to ask about the father of her baby, why she was living back here, how long before she left again, if she was happy. Instead, he looked out the windscreen and went for, 'How are your parents? Your dad still flying?'

At first it seemed she had no intention of answering. But just when he was about to try again she answered. 'Dad's set to retire at the end of the year. He's getting tired of long-haul flights, finds each one a little harder to recover from than the last. But he doesn't want to go back on the domestic route. Says that's for the up-and-coming pilots to sharpen their teeth on.'

'I've never understood how pilots manage all those hours in the air, their bodies not really coping with all the time-zone changes. It can't be good in the long run.' Yet he remembered Ian Wilson always having abundant energy. Working their avocado and citrus orchards when he was at home, going fishing, flying his plane, taking his family away for hiking weekends. He'd never stopped. His daughter had the same genes.

'You haven't seen Dad for a while. He's looking older. And he doesn't move as fast any more.' Sadness laced her statement. 'He's only sixty-three, for goodness' sake. He shouldn't be slowing down.'

'Are you worried about it? Enough to suggest he see a doctor?'

'No, it's life catching up, I think.' She changed gear to reduce speed for a sharp bend. 'Jackson's working in Hong Kong so they catch up whenever Dad flies that way.'

So Dr Jackson Wilson, Sasha's older brother, now lived halfway round the world. No surprise. The guy had been in a hurry to leave the bay the moment he'd finished high school. Guess he hadn't stopped when he'd reached Auckland either. 'What does your mother think about Ian retiring?'

'She's the reason he's not stopping as soon as he'd like. I think she's afraid he'll take over her orchard and leave her with little to do.'

'Hardly surprising. It's been her baby for years.'

Again Sash went all quiet on him. This time the silence hung heavily between them as she concentrated on negotiating the final hairpin bend, her eyes focused straight ahead, her lips pressed hard together. He sensed the tension in her thighs, arms and the rest of her compact body. Because of the road conditions? Or the fact he'd used the baby word?

He broke the silence. 'When I went for a walk yesterday I noticed the orchard's been expanded. There's a lot of work there for anyone to cope with.' If Ian was sixty-three then his wife had to be a similar age. Time to relax a bit, surely?

It took a few minutes but finally she answered so quietly he had to strain to hear her. 'Mum tries, and I help when I can.'

'Is that wise in your condition? Orchard work's quite heavy.' Seemed his runaway tongue had no problem with talking. Then his head jerked forward as the car skated to an abrupt halt.

'By the time you've walked home you might've learned to keep your unwanted opinions to yourself.' Sasha stared out the windscreen, not even dignifying him with a glare.

'I'm sorry. Again.' He waited. He had no intention of getting out into the night and waiting for the unlikely event of another vehicle coming along.

Might try and learn to keep your trap shut while you're waiting. Because up until now it's done nothing but get you further than ever offside with Sasha. If that was possible.

Something akin to fear slithered under his skin. What if he never got to laugh with Sasha again? Never saw her eyes light up into that brilliant summer green that hit him right in the heart? Could he still go and knock on her door and say hi?

She wouldn't need that from him. Those bases would be covered with the father of her baby. Nausea rolled up Grady's throat. He hadn't been able to do any of those things for years. Long, lonely years when he'd looked for her in every woman he dated.

Suddenly he really, truly, understood how coming back to Golden Bay had little to do with working on his house. He could've paid a carpenter to do that. No, this mad idea had been all about Sasha and their past.

But it had to be friendship he was looking for.

Nope. Not at all. But it was all he'd get.

But first he needed a ride home.

He did the one thing he was very good at, had been doing for years. He waited.

CHAPTER THREE

SASHA SNAPPED THE shower off after a quick soap and sluice job and snatched at her towel. She'd slept in. She'd be late for work. The one thing she'd do anything to avoid. And on a Monday morning it'd be bedlam at the medical centre. Hopefully, Mike and Roz would give her some slack because she'd been helping Sam and Lucy. There'd be no problem with Rory. He was more laid back than his medical partners.

Why hadn't she heard her alarm? Hard to believe she'd fallen asleep the moment her head had touched the pillow, that there hadn't been hours of tossing and turning while Grady ran amok in her skull.

But the moment her eyes had popped open this morning he'd been there. That wary, lopsided smile clawing at her heartstrings. His gravelly voice thrilling her deep, deep inside, stirring hormones into a dance. The lid had lifted off that memory box again.

'Grady O'Neil, I've missed you so much.' Nothing or nobody in the intervening years had filled the hole he'd torn out of her heart. Out of her soul. There'd been men, for sure, but none had touched her as deeply as Grady. Not even greaseball had hurt her as badly. Could be she was getting used to being tossed aside by the men she'd cared about. Thank goodness. She wouldn't have survived a repeat of the kind of devastation Grady had caused, leaving her hollowed out.

Kick, kick.

Until the advent of her baby. Flipper would go a long way to making her feel complete again. Flipper would soak up all the love she had to give. 'My baby girl.'

Swiping the condensation off the mirror, Sasha studied her belly. So round, smooth, life-giving. Her fingers splayed across the taut skin and she turned sideways for a different view. 'Oh, wow.' Tears misted her eyes, clogged her throat. 'You're beautiful already.'

She never tired of this view. Pregnancy had

turned out to be amazing. Hard to believe that a wee baby girl was growing in there, getting ready for the big, wide world. What colour were her eyes? Her hair? 'My baby. My love.' Sniff. 'I promise you, Flipper, I'm going to be the best darned mother you'd ever wish for.' Sniff. 'I love you so much already.' Would love cover all her failings? Help her make wise decisions regarding just about everything? Would her love make up for the lack of a father?

Tossing the towel in the general direction of the drying rail, Sasha fumbled for a tissue and blew hard.

No, Grady, the job's not up for grabs. As much as my baby needs a dad, I'm not letting you in. It's bad enough you shoved my love back in my face, and on a bad day I might even take another chance on you, admit extenuating circumstances, but what if you left again? That could hurt Flipper, which is non-negotiable. So, byebye, Grady.

But, for the record, her real father's out of the picture, too. He made it clearer than a fine winter's day that he wants absolutely nothing to do with this child. As far as I'm concerned, he's had his chance.

Kick.

'Hey, baby girl. You should be sleeping in after your late night.' Dropping the soggy tissue in the waste basket, Sasha picked up her knickers and stepped into them. Reached for her bra, which got tighter by the day. 'You know we're running late, Flipper? The centre will be buzzing with people who've knocked themselves about over the weekend, playing rugby or netball, plus the usual line-up of colds and flu.' The zip on her pregnancy trousers caught. 'Flipper, you're putting on weight.'

As she shoved her arms into her blouse there was a loud pounding on her front door. 'Who the heck?' Just what she needed, a visitor when she should already be on the road. Then she relaxed. It'd be Jessica. There'd been a message on the answering-machine when she'd got in to call her friend urgently, no matter what the time of day or night. Fairly certain Jessica would be phoning to warn her about Grady's reappearance, she'd opted to wait until she saw her at work rather than talk for what had been left of the night about how to deal with him.

Heading for the front of her cottage, she left buttoning her blouse and tugged on a woollen cardigan. She swung the door wide, shivering in the cold blast that immediately whacked her. 'Hey, you can save your breath. I already...' Her voice petered out as her eyes encountered the one person she'd never expected to see at this moment.

'You already what?' Grady asked in such a normal tone, like he always dropped by her place, that the temperature of her blood went from normal to boiling in a flash.

Remain calm. Breathe deep. 'What are you doing here?'

Grady's eyes widened but otherwise he remained unperturbed. 'I need a ride to the medical centre. My car's at Mike's.' His hand slid through that wonderful, nearly shoulder-length black hair that she refused to remember running her fingers through. 'I presume you're heading that way shortly.'

The heat in her veins evaporated immediately.

A ride to the centre? In her car? He was doing something so mundane as asking a neighbour for a lift and yet she wanted to yell no at him. Yearned to close her door in his beautiful face and lean back on it, while pretending that the guy on the other side meant no more to her than yesterday's lunch. So much for not letting Grady get to her.

Be calm, act rationally. Do the right, the sensible thing. 'No problem. Give me a minute. I'll grab my jacket and bag.' She didn't try to sound chirpy. Too tired for that. And wired. Grady mightn't have kept her awake last night but she hadn't forgotten for an instant that she'd seen him, that he was back, that she'd *missed him* more than she'd ever guessed. That her body went a little crazy whenever he was near. Shouldn't pregnancy dull the sex buzz?

A buzz he didn't seem to be feeling as he said, 'Thanks. I'm covering for Mike this morning while he catches up on much-needed sleep. They didn't get back from Nelson until about five.'

The vague hope that she could drive fast, dump Grady at Mike's and get on with her day vanished. They'd be in the same building most of the morning until she headed off on her rounds. She'd be unable to avoid him. Even if she didn't see him she'd hear his deep voice when he talked with patients as he led them to his consulting room or when he took a coffee break in the kitchen. So? What happened to doing friendly? Grady seemed to be managing that. Surely she could? Or didn't he feel anything about the past? Had he got over it so well that he really thought friendship was possible?

Get real. Grady told you he didn't love you any more. What was there to get over?

Spinning on her heel, she left him on the doorstep and headed for the kitchen to collect her gear and something to have for breakfast once she got to work.

'Sash,' he called after her.

Spinning back, she glared at him, holding in the pain that using the diminutive form of her name caused. Today she would not lower herself to plead that he refrain from using it. Instead, she slapped a hand on her hip and, barely resisting tapping her foot, waited.

'Sorry. Sasha.' His chest lifted, fell back into place under that navy jersey that fitted him like a second skin, accentuating all the details of his chest she'd prefer to forget. The tip of his tongue appeared at the corner of his mouth. 'You might want to take a few more minutes and finish getting dressed.'

What? She glanced downwards. Great. Her blouse was only half-buttoned, exposing her new, getting-bigger-by-the-day cleavage. Her feet were bare. Heck, she hadn't put any make-up on yet or done her hair. 'Make that ten minutes.'

Grady watched as Sash did that spin-on-her-heel thing again. Her back was straighter than straight, her long, mussed hair bouncing as she charged away. And his belly squeezed hard on the boiled egg he'd eaten half an hour ago. Did those golden locks still feel like silk? Did she still enjoy having them hand-combed by someone else?

The wind roared across the lawn, pelted his back with cold and knocked the door against the wall. He stepped inside and closed winter out. Now what? Did he wander through the house like he was welcome? Or wait here just inside the door like a nervous kid outside the headmaster's office? Like he'd ever done that.

He strode towards the door opposite where Sash had disappeared, hopeful of finding the kitchen. What if her partner was there? Then he'd front up, introduce himself and explain why he was here. He would not say he'd deliberately come by to meet him, to find out who he was and see if they already knew each other.

That baby bump was still there, hadn't disappeared overnight. Hadn't been a figment of his overactive imagination. Breakfast rolled over. Regurgitated egg tasted disgusting. Hadn't tasted that flash first time round, come to think of it. He'd eaten on autopilot, knowing he'd regret it later if he didn't have breakfast but not overly interested in what he ate. His head space had been filled with images from last night of Sash. Angry, cautious, smiling—not at him—shocked, and very, very protective of her unborn child.

The cupboard that was obviously the kitchen was empty. No partner here. Grady didn't know whether to feel relieved or disappointed. The moment of reckoning had only been delayed.

'Right, let's go.' Sasha's hand appeared in the periphery of his vision as she snatched up keys lying on the bench.

'Sasha.' Grady knew he should stop right there but the words kept on coming. 'Do you live here alone?'

'Yes,' she called over her shoulder, as she strode away to the front door. Her hand on the door handle tightened then she whipped around to face him, her annoyed-looking eyes locking with his. 'Yes,' she repeated more emphatically. And then she waited, apparently understanding what he wanted to know and not making it easy for him.

'The baby's father doesn't live with you?' *What part of living alone didn't you get?*

'Definitely not,' she snapped, then blinked and turned away, tugging the door open, but not before he saw anger flicker across her face, widening her eyes.

Not sure how he should be feeling right now, he followed her outside. If there wasn't a father in the picture then maybe he could spend some time getting alongside her and see where that led. Probably fooling himself, setting himself up for heartbreak.

What about that baby? Do you want to be a part of its life? Because if you're wanting Sash back then she comes with extras.

Something to think about. Though his need to get alongside Sash might override any concerns about the child. At the moment, anyway.

Watching her closely as those keys she'd snatched up flew from one ring-laden hand to the other and back while she waited for him to come outside, he had to resist the urge to wrap her up in a big hug. Nothing sexual. A completely caring and friendly embrace. A hug to take away some of that despair she was valiantly trying to hide behind anger.

The front door closed with a bang. Then the locks on that canary-yellow car popped. Sash's feet slapped hard on the pavement as she closed the gap to her vehicle then swung back to face him. She'd applied make-up in those few minutes she'd left him standing around, yet her face appeared ghostly pale. But her spine had clicked dead straight again.

'I am going to be a solo mother.' Fierce words spoken in her don't-screw-with-me attitude. So Sash. Watch out anyone who gave her a hard time over that. And there'd be plenty. Small communities might turn out to support anyone who needed them but there was always the gossip doing the rounds, too. Which was why her brother had left so long ago.

'I'm sorry to hear that.' And he was. He mightn't like another man in her life but he was big enough to acknowledge single parenthood would be no easy feat and he really didn't want Sasha having to face it alone.

'Don't be. It's for the best.' She slid into the car and shoved the key into the ignition. 'Coming?'

Why did I just tell Grady that? It's absolutely none of his business. At the gate Sasha lifted her foot off the brake too quickly and the vehicle jerked forward. *It's not a secret. Probably best to put it out there so he's not badgering me with more questions.*

When she'd spilled the truth there'd been something in Grady's eyes that had curled her toes with warmth, as though he was on her side. Which had to be the dumbest thought she'd had in a long time. Why would he be? And why had the idea of Grady being there for her in any way, shape or form made her feel a smidgeon better than she had five minutes ago?

She *was* doing this alone. Jessica, as friend and midwife, would see her through the pregnancy and birth, but the hard yards were all down to her. Her parents would always stand by her, but in the end the baby was her responsibility. *Hope I know what I'm doing, Flipper.* Her hand dropped to her extended belly and did a quick lap over the bump.

Unable to stop herself, she glanced sideways, met Grady's steady gaze, saw wonder all mixed up with yearning gleaming out at her. Oh—my—goodness. A sensation in her chest of something like a mouse on a treadmill brought tears bursting into her eyes. Her neck clicked as she flicked her head forward, taking her eyes away from that unrealistic sight.

If only that picture was for real, like they were a happy couple expecting their first child. It should be true, would've been if he hadn't dumped her. Grady would make an awesome dad. But not for her little girl. Flipper was not going to grow up believing Grady would always be there for her only to discover he left when she wasn't looking.

Back up. Grady had put his mother and sisters before her, before them. His family had desperately needed his undivided attention and support at the time. He'd also put training to become a doctor on hold. It hadn't only been about not wanting her. With Mum's illness beginning to make an impact on her family's lives she was beginning to understand what he'd been facing. But he should've talked to her, told her everything. Shared his problems.

Toot, toot. A car pulled up beside her vehicle, stopping in the middle of the road. Sasha looked out. Mum's head was poking out of the driver's window, surprise widening her eyes as she peered past her. Oh, great. Now for the forty questions.

Best cut her off at the pass. 'Hey, Mum, how's

things? I'll have to find someone else to take the lemons over the hill tonight. Lucy and Sam had an accident last night and are in hospital so I'm not sure what's happening with their freight run.' *Shut up. You're babbling.* Anyway, Mum hadn't heard a word, she was too busy sussing out the man sitting beside her.

'Grady, it's good to see you. I heard you were at the house, and hoped to catch up with you in the next day or two to ask you over for a meal. Ian will be back tonight. Sasha's joining us for dinner tomorrow so how about you come along?' Now who was babbling? At least Mum hadn't said it would be just like old times. Yet. 'It would be—'

Sasha held her breath.

Mum continued, 'Lovely to catch up with what you've been up to since we last saw you.'

Thanks for the loyalty, Mum. Where was the 'Who the heck do you think you are, coming back here when Sasha's finally moved back home?'

Grady leaned forward, shot a quick look at Sasha that told her exactly what he was going to say. 'Hello, Virginia. I'd love to catch up with you and Ian. I'll bring a bottle of wine.'

'Lovely.' Mum beamed. Mothers had no right to invite ex-boyfriends to dinner. They should know better. But, then, Mum hadn't really seen the devastation Grady's defection had wrought on her, hadn't known that she'd gone from wild to wilder for twelve months. Hadn't known how many pieces her heart had broken into and how, when it had come to putting it back together, it had been like a jigsaw with bits missing.

Sasha swallowed her annoyance. 'Mum, did you hear me? Lucy and Sam crashed their truck last night. They're in hospital.'

Finally Mum's attention flipped to her. 'What? That's terrible. How badly hurt are they? I'll go over and see to the chooks and dogs.'

'Leave it, Mum. I'll see to that after work.'

She got a glare for an answer.

'Mr and Mrs Donovan will be in hospital for a few days,' Grady informed them. 'Mike says their injuries are not serious.'

Repeating herself, Sasha said, 'I'll ring the other carriers and see if we can get the citrus cases picked up from your shed. Otherwise I'll load them after work and take them into the depot.' The fruit needed to be at the market early tomorrow morning. 'But right now I'm late for work. See you later.'

Putting the vehicle in gear, she slowly drove away. Mum looked more tired than usual this morning. Thank goodness Dad was nearly home. He'd be able to do some of those jobs Mum insisted she was still capable of doing. Like driving into the township for supplies. Like loading heavy cases onto the ute and delivering them to the depot. Which was definitely *her* job whenever Mum would listen.

She hated this illness; hated the thought Mum would slowly lose the ability to do all the things she loved doing. Mothers weren't meant to get ill. They were meant to be there for ever. *Well, I'm going to be here for ever, watching, helping, looking after her. Doing everything possible to make life easier for her.*

She'd ring Mum later and see if she needed anything picked up. Grady was in for a shock tomorrow night. By the end of the day her mother didn't always have the strength for cooking so they could very well get heat and eat on a foil plate. Nothing like the wonderful home-cooked meals Mum used to be famous for in Takaka.

Deep in thought, she hadn't noticed the silence in the cab until Grady broke it with, 'You're annoyed I accepted your mother's invitation.'

Was she? Probably. Seemed he was getting into her space too much, too quickly. 'A little. But I'll get over it.' Please.

'I can beg off if you want me to.'

'Leave it, Grady. Mum would be disappointed. Just…' How did she explain without explaining?

'Sasha? Is everything okay? You and the baby are doing fine, aren't you?' Talk about a left-field question. How did he go from discussing her mother to asking about her baby? His concern could be her undoing. If she let it.

Her lips pressed together and her eyes blurred as hurt for Mum gripped her. Blinking furiously, she focused on the road in front, thankful for the lack of traffic at this time of year. Shaking her head from side to side, she managed, 'Everything's hunky-dory. But it can be a little out of whack at times so be prepared for anything tomorrow.'

And that was all he was getting. The ache in the back of her throat grew but at least her vision cleared. She could feel Grady watching her closely. There'd be questions in those beautiful eyes that always saw too much. She would not look at him. There was plenty of time later if she wanted to talk to him about the disease devastating her family. And whether she did or didn't depended on lots of things, but mainly on how well they got along over the next few days.

Grady had skin thicker than the steers she could see in the paddock alongside the road. 'What's this about you loading the boxes of lemons? You can't do that in your condition.'

Condition? Like I'm sick or something. 'Trust me. I won't do anything that could hurt my baby.'

'I believe you, but do you recognise when you're doing too much? I remember those boxes. They weren't light. You should leave the job to someone else.'

Like who? 'When did you turn so bossy?'

'I had two teenage sisters to deal with. They never made anything easy for me. I probably didn't make it easy for them either, trying to fill

Dad's shoes and be the man about the place. I wasn't ready for that job.'

'It must've been hell for you all.' She relaxed, tossed him a smile. 'But go, them. Where are they these days?'

'They're both in London with Ma and her husband. Collete's a lawyer and Eve's a gym instructor.'

'Your mother remarried?'

'Yes, two years after Dad died.' His tone quietened, deepened.

'That didn't make you happy?'

'I'm fine with it. Carrington's a good man and Ma's blissfully happy. She's not the kind of woman who can live on her own for long. She doesn't cope well with finances and making sure the insurance or rates are paid.' His turn to stare out the window at the passing paddocks. 'That took me a while to realise and when I did she'd made some bad calls with money. She wouldn't let me take total control so we agreed to sell the trucking business and invest the money to give her a monthly payment. It worked, sort of. Then along came Carrington and he took care of them all.'

'Leaving you free to get on with your medical training.'

'I took the remaining six months of that year off, went north to pick fruit, tried my hand on a commercial fishing trawler, pulled beers in a pub. Generally let loose for a while, knowing that once I started at med school there'd be no let-up for a long time.'

'Makes sense.' While Grady was okay with talking about himself she'd absorb every detail going. It was getting harder by the minute to keep him at arm's length. She craved information about him, what he'd done, where he'd lived, who he loved.

Who Grady loved? Did he have a partner? Was she in Auckland, working while he dealt with this pesky little issue of a house out in the back of nowhere? Her heart rate picked up speed. What did any of that matter? She wasn't getting back with the guy and she'd be the last person to wish him anything but happiness.

With relief she pulled into the car park at the back of the medical centre. At least there'd be more air in the centre, fresh air that didn't hold that spicy scent that was Grady, and she wouldn't starve for oxygen because he'd sucked it all up.

'There you go. Delivered safe and sound.' Wasn't that what Jessica would say when she put Flipper in her arms? Giving Grady a ride had seemed almost as traumatic, though not as painful.

'So uneventful I thought I was dreaming.' A hint of laughter in his voice had her head spinning round. He added, 'I don't remember a single time you ever drove or flew me anywhere that was downright steady and safe.'

Yeah, she'd been a little on the wild side then, had got worse after their bust-up. 'That was before Flipper.' Long, long before. Recently life had become so sedate she bored herself.

'Flipper?' His mouth twitched into a heart-wrenching smile.

'Baby. Commonly known as Flipper for her swimming antics that feel like what I've seen the dolphins doing out in the bay, rising and falling through the water.'

'Her? So you're having a girl.' His smile died, his gaze turned wistful. 'A little Sasha.'

Why wistful? This was her, the woman he'd professed not to love, at least not enough to hang around with for the rest of his life. 'Yep, a little me. Guess I'm in for payback time for all the worry I put my parents through. Dad keeps warning me I'll have heart failure every time she moves, wondering what antics she'll get up to and if she'll be safe.'

'Ian encouraged you to do those things. It was your mother who had the heart failure.' Thank goodness the laughter had returned to his voice. She didn't like Grady being sad. It didn't fit her memories, the ones that had escaped the box overnight.

He'd always been full of fun and laughter, teasing, happy. Ping. Another memory. The day his father had dropped dead on the golf course. Grady had never been Grady afterwards. The shock had knocked him and his mother and two much younger sisters to their knees. Mr O'Neil's passing had been completely unexpected. He hadn't had a sick day in all his adult life. Never been to a doctor. Hadn't swallowed pills for anything. A big, solid man, who'd adored his family, worked hard and given generously. Died at forty-four of a massive coronary while swinging an iron at a golf ball.

When Sasha had heard the appalling news she'd gone home and hugged her dad hard and long. It had been impossible to imagine what losing a parent would be like, but she'd known how much she'd loved Mum and Dad and had never stopped telling and showing them ever since.

That day had been the beginning of the changes that had overtaken her and Grady's lives. What if she'd been too impatient with him? Selfish in her own wants, not hearing beyond what he'd actually said? She'd moved on, trained as a nurse, done pretty much anything and everything she'd wanted, and now was preparing for a new challenge—becoming a mum. But what if she'd failed Grady? Was that why men left her? Because she didn't stack up when the chips were down?

The sound of a car door slamming broke into her reverie and reminded her she was already late. At least Mike wasn't here to give her a hard time about that, and Roz might just be more relaxed and prepared to give her a chance after last night's events. 'Better get cracking. Monday mornings are hectic, without fail.'

She didn't wait for Grady but headed straight inside, anxious to put some space between them. Until last night she hadn't considered if bringing up Flipper alone was wrong. Sure, all kids needed two parents, and that was on a good day, but those who only got one seemed to do okay. Until Grady's reappearance she hadn't worried too much about that.

CHAPTER FOUR

'HEY, YOU DIDN'T call me.' Jessica looked up from her desk in the nurses' office as Sasha slipped inside and opened her locker.

'Get growled at for waking you at two in the morning? I don't live that dangerously. Any more,' she added under her breath.

Jessica fixed her with a compassionate look. 'Sasha, I want to warn you…' She hesitated.

Sasha dived straight in. 'Grady's back.'

'You know? Who told you? No one at the medical centre knows about your past with him.'

Sasha's lips flattened. 'I had the privilege of giving him a ride home in the early hours. I came across the Donovans caught inside their truck after sliding off the road last night and when the rescue crews turned up, guess who lined up with them?' Shrugging out of her jacket, she went for broke. 'I've also brought him into work as he's covering for Mike this morning.'

'You okay with this?' Jessica's chair scraped the floor as she pushed it back to stand.

'Do I have a choice?' The hand hanging up the jacket shook hard. No, she wasn't okay. About Grady's reappearance in her home town. About him coming to dinner at her parents' home, like old times. About him working at her workplace. About anything.

Jess's arms surrounded her, pulled her in for a hug. 'Want to take a sickie?' she whispered.

'A four-week one? Yep, I do.' Which only showed how rattled Grady made her feel because she never, ever ducked for cover when the going got tough. Hadn't had it this tough for a while, though.

Stepping away, Jessica gave her a twisted smile. 'Which doctor will you ask to sign the leave form? Roz or Rory? Or Grady?'

'Now, there's a thought.' Retrieving her yoghurt and fruit to put in the fridge, she asked, 'Want a coffee before mayhem arrives?'

'Too late. It's already here. You've got a stack of patient files higher than my dirty dishes at home.'

'Then I'm never going to get done today.'

'Let's go grab that coffee anyway.' Jessica led the way to the kitchen. 'Bet you haven't eaten this morning.'

'You know me too well.'

'Eat that yoghurt and banana before you start work.'

'Why is it that because I'm pregnant everyone thinks they can tell me what to do? You're not the first today.'

'Let me guess. Grady been giving you orders, too?' Jess actually smiled around her question.

Traitor. 'Don't act like that's a good thing,' Sasha said as she tugged the foil off the yoghurt pot. Because it was out of order. He had no place in her life. And her friend's role was to support her, no matter what.

Jessica's smile widened. 'Mrs Collins is waiting for you to take her stitches out. Brought us a chocolate cake for morning tea as well. Which is good because that's not enough breakfast for you and your baby.'

'Chocolate cake?' The thought of it made her gag. And she wasn't insulting Mrs Collins's cooking. Those chocolate cakes she made were the best on the planet. If only her stomach wasn't in a riot of nerves. 'Flipper might like some.'

Jess threaded her arm through Sasha's. 'How is my favourite baby?'

'Bet you say that to all your mothers.'

'Of course I do.'

'Cheers.' One of the best things to come out of returning home to have her baby was discovering that Jessica had also returned to Golden Bay only weeks earlier and would be her midwife. She couldn't think of anyone better to be there when she delivered. They were forging a strong friendship. Jess had been in Jackson's year at school so they hadn't known each other well. Jess's family life had been hectic and chaotic back then.

Inside the kitchen Sasha stopped, suddenly overwhelmed by everything. She studied her hands as she asked quietly, 'Jessica, I am going to manage, aren't I?' She swallowed a huge lump that had risen to block her throat. 'I know nothing about bringing up a child. Apart from my nursing training I haven't had anything to do with babies. What if I make a right royal mess of things? Get the award for worst mother of the year? Flipper will grow up hating me.' She blinked as moisture threatened to spill down her cheeks.

'You? Worst mother? Not possible. You haven't got a hopeless cell in your body.'

'Every cell feels more than hopeless at the moment.' This debilitating sensation hadn't happened before. Until this morning she'd been quietly confident she'd get parenting mostly right, and if she got stuck she had her own great parents to turn to. Even with the problems they were facing at the moment, they couldn't wait to be grandparents. Staring at her shaking hands, she almost cried. 'What's come over me?'

Jessica hugged her. 'You're hormonal. It's quite normal in your condition. I was a blithering idiot at six months.'

'Hormonal? That covers a multitude of things.' And ignored what might be the real reason for her distress. That man she'd brought to work with her. Hugging Jessica back, she stepped away, headed for the kettle, plastering a false smile on her dial and bracing herself for the day.

'Did you bring photos of the wedding with you?' Jess asked.

Duh, of course. 'The camera's in my bag.'

'I'll grab it. Can't wait to see Tina in all her finery.'

'She looked gorgeous,' Sasha said, the moment Jessica stepped back into the kitchen. 'Stunning, as did Paolo. And when they said their vows I cried.' Just like she was doing now. Fat, silent tears rolled down her cheeks. 'They are so happy, so in love, it's like magic.' Her heart swelled with emotion. 'It was the most beautiful wedding I've ever been to. They walked under an arch of skis and the theme of the reception was all about skiing.'

'I should learn to ski and go to Italy, find myself a gorgeous Italian man like Tina did.'

'Didn't work for me.' Sasha smiled genuinely at last.

Jess held the camera in one hand, deftly clicking through the photos, and wrapped her free arm around Sasha's shoulders. 'Hey, the bridesmaid looked gorgeous, too. That shade of emerald really suits her.'

'I tried to hide the bump as much as possible but it wasn't easy.' Sasha hiccupped and dashed at her cheeks with the back of her hand. 'Tina kept telling me to stop worrying but most of her wedding photos are going to have my pregnant belly as the centre of attention.'

Jess squeezed her shoulder. 'If Tina hadn't wanted Flipper in her photos she'd have taken you up on your suggestion she find another bridesmaid. She's a true friend.'

More tears fell. 'I'm a right mess this morning,' she muttered as she sniffed hard.

'Babymones.' Jess grinned around her made-up word for pregnancy hormones. Then the grin slipped as she leaned close. 'And a little bit of disturbance in the two-metre package that just walked past the door.'

'I wish…' Sasha hauled in a deep breath. 'You know, I haven't a clue what I wish when it comes to Grady. I seem to be having some positive thoughts, memories…' Again her voice trailed off and she shrugged.

'You've got Flipper to think about. Leave Grady to his own resources. And if it gets too bad you come see me. Okay?'

'Okay.' She was so lucky with her friends. They really cared about her. As she did them. Tina had insisted she be bridesmaid, saying after all the things they'd done together during the two years they'd nursed in Dubai the small matter of a baby wasn't going to stop her having Sasha beside her as she said her marriage vows.

And now Jessica and her little boy, Nicholas, had become an integral part of her life. She really had nothing to complain about, and everything she could wish for.

Except a father for her baby.

Grady tapped his fingers on the top of Mike's desk. George Browning had gone, happy with a prescription for his cholesterol and something to clear his chest infection.

He should be heading out to the waiting room to collect the next patient but he needed a moment. He'd overheard Sasha talking to Jess in the kitchen, heard the raw uncertainty in her voice.

So unlike the Sash he remembered. From the highest hair on her head to the ends of her toes she'd always emanated confidence. Always. Too much sometimes, but that was better than not enough.

Admittedly, being responsible for a tiny baby had to be different. Scary. Daunting. Especially doing it on her own. His fingers shoved through his hair. Sasha was having a baby. It still rocked him to think about it. And he'd thought about it for what had been left of the night after she'd dropped him off at his house. Sasha Wilson. Once the love of his life. *You are still capable of rattling me, turning my heart upside down, making me want you and to be a part of your life.*

Grady visualised Sasha holding her baby, crooning sweet nothings, placing delicate kisses on her forehead. She'd throw herself full on into motherhood, as she'd always done with anything. That baby she carried didn't know yet how lucky she was to have Sasha for a mum. If he ever had kids, their mother would have to be just like her.

Just like her? Or her?

His hand clenched, banged down on the desk.

His mouth dried. Yeah, sure, Sasha having his kids? After the way he'd treated her?

'Knock, knock. Are you all right?' Roz appeared in his line of vision, a worried look on her face.

Forcing a smile, he leaned back in the chair. 'Absolutely.'

'I just wanted to say thanks for stepping in for Mike. He's been putting in some long hours lately and getting quite exhausted. Last night didn't help.' Roz parked her backside on the corner of the desk.

'You're welcome. I didn't feel very excited about painting this morning anyway.' He'd taken one look at the boring off-white colour and banged the lid back on the tin. That house needed vibrant colours to bring it alive again. It needed people. Laughter echoing in the rooms. Music playing in the background. Which was why he was selling it, remember?

'Where have you gone?' Roz knocked on the desktop.

'Sorry. I'm happy to help you and Mike out further if either of you need a break.'

Roz grinned like she'd got something she wanted. 'We'll take you up on that.' Her finger scratched at the desktop. 'Having you here won't be a problem for Sasha? I didn't realise until Mike said something about it this morning that you two had history.'

'No.' He hoped not. 'It's very old history. We met when I used to come over here for summer holidays but until last night I hadn't seen her since the year she left school and Golden Bay. My family never came back here after that summer either.' Too many memories of Dad for all of them to cope with. And, for him, memories of Sash.

Roz stood and smoothed down her skirt. 'Can I ask you something? Just in case she annoys you or does something irritating? Can you go easy on her? There are a lot of things going on in her life at the moment and she's very fragile.'

'Sure.' Sash fragile? She'd always been strong. He stared at Roz, hoping for an explanation, but the woman was heading for the door.

One of us doesn't know Sash very well. Was that Roz? Or was it him? Did this explain the need to hug and protect Sasha he'd felt last night? And again this morning when he'd knocked on her door and found her in a dishevelled state? It was a gut-level feeling that gripped him whenever she came close. A feeling he'd never had for her before.

Earlier, when he'd heard Sash ask Jessica about her coping skills, he'd wanted to rush in and yell, 'Yes, of course you'll do a fantastic job.' He'd wanted to hug her tight to keep those fears at bay. As if she'd listen to him. But she'd sounded so frightened. Alone, even, despite the midwife being there for her. He'd be the last person Sasha would want overhearing that short conversation, let alone offering comfort.

Anyway, what did he know about raising a child? Grady could hear the distain colouring her voice now. She'd really get stuck into him. And he'd had enough of that from her last night. Even if he had deserved it.

'Got a moment, Grady?' Sasha appeared in the doorway.

This office was busier than a bus station. 'Got a problem?' he asked.

Her green gaze cruised over him while her mouth lifted and dropped as though she hadn't made up her mind how to treat him.

'Go for friendly.' He smiled broadly, practising what he preached.

She blinked, squinted at him. Her shoulders rose and fell quickly. 'Is there any other way?' But her return smile was kind of sad.

'You wanted me?' Or a doctor?

'Can you take a look at Mrs Collins for me? She came in to have stitches removed from a gash in her left calf muscle. Apparently she had an accident while chopping wood last week. The wound is inflamed and oozing. She needs a new prescription for antibiotics.'

So Sasha wanted a doctor, not him. Get used to it. She was setting the tone for the rest of his time here.

Didn't mean he had to take any notice, did it?

The stars were beginning to show by the time Sasha turned into the orchard's drive and headed for the packing shed. She ached with exhaustion. It had been a long, hard day following a long, hard night. Her last patient, nearly an hour away out past Collingwood, had been in need of some TLC more than anything medical. She'd changed a dressing and drunk milky tea and eaten week-old lemon cake.

Ruth Cornwell lived in the falling-down house she'd been born in seventy-nine years ago, and no one would be getting her out of there unless it was in a box. Ruth's words, which Sasha had heard on numerous occasions, today being no exception. A tough old lady, she was now very lonely after falling out with most of her neighbours over the years. But suggest she move into a rest home? You'd better be able to run fast.

'Okay, Flipper, let's get those lemons loaded. Then we can take them to the carrier's yard before heading home for a hot shower and dinner.'

Dinner. Her shoulders slumped. She hadn't been to the supermarket, and her cupboard was bare. A yawn dragged her mouth wide. If it weren't for Flipper she'd head home, eat the last yoghurt and fall into bed. But she shouldn't be doing that. Bad mummy practice.

Just inside the shed door she patted the wall,

found the light switches and filled the space with light. And gaped. Where were all those cartons Mum had presumably packed over the weekend? They should be stacked by the bench for Sam Donovan to pick up. Mum had better not have taken them to the yard. She'd been warned time after time by Mike and her and Dad: do not lift those full boxes. 'Mum, I love you to bits, but you are so in trouble right now.'

The gravel on the driveway crunched and head-lights swung across the yard. Mum's ute turned into the carport at the side of the shed.

'Right, Mum, we're about to have a talk.' Switching on the outside lights, Sasha stomped outside and followed the side of the shed to the carport. But even as her mouth opened she was hauling on the brakes to halt her words.

Grady was locking the ute's door. He had a laden grocery bag swinging from one hand. He'd also changed in to butt-hugging jeans and a thick, woollen outdoors shirt with a roll-collar jersey underneath. Drop-dead gorgeous. Except Sasha felt she might be the one to drop dead with the need unfurling deep inside her. Her swallow was audible in the quiet night.

'Hey, Sasha. I heard you were going to be late back so I dropped those cases off at the depot. Hope that's okay?'

As he approached, the need to lean into him and let him take over for an hour or two nearly floored her. Click, click, her back straightened with difficulty. 'Sure. Thank you.' Try again, Sasha. That was feeble. 'I mean it, Grady. I am grateful. I hadn't been looking forward to loading up and going back into town.'

'I'm not surprised. Whenever I've seen you today you've looked shattered. Not enough sleep last night, huh?'

'That and a big weekend.' Maybe that yoghurt would have to do tonight. Unless she raided Mum's pantry before going home.

'You still like pasta?' Grady seemed to be holding his breath as he waited for her answer.

'I love it. Especially spaghetti carbonara.' That yoghurt seemed very unappetising now.

His hand delved into the bag, brought out a package. 'With bacon?'

Her mouth watered as she nodded.

'And cream?'

'If you're teasing me, Grady O'Neil, you'd better start running for the hills.' What was he up to? They'd managed to keep their distance all morning at the medical centre, acting polite and friendly in an aloof kind of way.

'I'm scrounging a ride home. Again. I'll cook you dinner.'

She swallowed, blinked back the tears threatening to spill over. 'Your house is five hundred metres from here. Oh…' She lightly slapped her forehead. 'It's dark and cold. Of course. Hop in and I'll run you home before the bogeyman comes up from the beach.'

Grady's laugh filled the chilly night air and lifted her heavy heart. For the first time all day she didn't feel held down with fear and need and the sense that time was running out. She also didn't feel that she should be avoiding Grady. Why she felt any of those things she had no idea. It was as though something was lurking on the periphery of her mind, worrying at her like a dog with its bone. But right now, here in her parents' yard, in the dark of nightfall and the cold of midwinter, she felt warm and safe. Felt she could cope with everything again. Why? She had no idea and wouldn't even try to find out.

Nothing to do with Grady, then? She certainly hoped not. Because even if she fell head over heels in love with him, what were the chances they could make it work? She carried another man's baby.

Backing the four-wheel drive round to face down the drive, she asked her passenger, 'Are you really putting your house on the market?'

Grady stretched his legs as far as they'd go under the console—not far at all. 'You've avoided the dinner question.'

And he'd avoided the house question. 'I should be making you dinner as a thank-you for taking those cases to the yard. But I'm guessing sharing a pot of yoghurt and a banana wouldn't cut it for you.' She eased on down to the road.

'We didn't used to thank each other for every little thing we did for the other.'

'We knew where we stood with each other back

then.' Why had she said that? Brought the elephant into the car? 'Forget I said that.'

'I will, on one condition. That you tell me whenever there's a stack of boxes to be loaded onto the ute for delivery. They weigh a lot for someone who's carrying a baby.' Grady's tone was still light and friendly but steel backed it.

'Dad's home tonight. He'll be doing the orchard jobs until his next trip.' Don't ask why Mum can't do it. I'm not ready to talk about that yet.

Thankfully he changed tack. Read her mind? Nah, it was a minefield in there and he looked relatively unscathed. 'Do you usually eat yoghurt every meal? I saw you scoffing some before you started work. I'd have thought you'd be into the fresh vegetables and salads, all the healthy stuff.'

'Anyone point out that it's winter and salad ingredients are hard to come by? When I do find them they're tasteless.'

'So carbonara it is.' So sure of himself. So— so friendly and ordinary. Ordinary in a 'we used to be lovers and now don't know what we are' sort of way.

'How can I turn down such an eloquent invitation?' Passing her cottage, she continued towards Pohara Beach and Grady's place, every metre of the way wondering if she'd just made a monumental blunder.

You're only going to eat a meal with the man. Not jump his bones.

Her vehicle jerked to the right. Grady reached over to grip the steering-wheel and straighten their direction. 'Sash?' There he went, one little word all full of heat, care and—sex.

Panic flared hard and fast. Her lungs worked overtime. 'I think I'll give the pasta a miss.' Coward. A total fraidy-cat.

'Your call.'

No pressure, then. Cool. He'd probably already decided he'd made a mistake by inviting her to share his meal. He had more sense than her at the moment. But she had babymones brain, remember? That was the best excuse for just about every darned mistake she made. Excuse? She needed an excuse to get out of spending an hour in Grady's house with him? Wouldn't it be better that she went and showed how little his return affected her? Show that the past was well and truly the past, that she didn't care enough to get all in a twitter whenever he was near?

Then Grady added, 'What does Flipper think about yoghurt for dinner when she could be having carbonara?'

Big pressure. 'Low blow, O'Neil.' But the panic had receded, replaced with soft warmth.

'Yep.'

Did he have to sound so smug? That alone should have her kicking him out of the vehicle and heading for home. She turned into his drive and stopped, looked around at the familiar and yet different yard. The lid snapped off the memory box. She shoved it back down tight. 'Looks like whoever lived here last didn't know much about lawnmowers.'

'Or hammering boards back on the fence. Or unblocking drains. Or cleaning the oven.'

'Got your work cut out, then.' Curiosity rose above the need to drop Grady and go. 'Is there a lot of damage around the place?'

Grady pushed his door wide. 'Mostly superficial but time-consuming. The family who rented it for ten years only came for holidays. Guess they didn't want to waste time doing any work around the place.' When he stood up she could no longer see his head or half his chest. Though those well-defined thighs were filling her vision and tickling up her senses a treat, sending her stomach into another riot—this time with desire. Then she heard him ask very casually, 'Come inside and I'll show you what I've got planned for the place.'

'As long as you remember my name is Sasha.'

CHAPTER FIVE

GRADY INTERNALISED HIS GRIN. Sash was rattled. That had to be good. If she didn't care two dots about him and them then she wouldn't give a rat's backside what he called her. But he'd hold back on overusing the Sash word, would endeavour to call her by her full name most of the time. Because first of all he needed to know her situation.

If she was head over heels in love with that baby's father then he would be out of the bay and on his way back to Auckland quicker than it took for the paint to dry on these walls. He might want her back in his arms but he'd never break up her relationship for his own needs. But if those often sad eyes were anything to go by, he doubted Sasha was in love. Unless it was unrequited love. His heart turned over for her. For him.

She'd followed him inside and now stood in the

open-plan living/dining/kitchen space, looking around as if searching for something.

He went for casual. 'I'll put a pot of water on to boil for the spaghetti before anything else.'

She didn't comment, merely walked across to the long wooden table and ran her hand over the now badly worn finish. If he'd been staying he'd have sanded it back to the wood and revarnished it. Sasha's look was wistful, snagging him in places he didn't want to be snagged. He could see the memories in her eyes, and felt his throat clogging as images he'd refused to think about over the last few days came roaring to the fore. Dad was in most of them.

'He loved it here, didn't he?' She knew he'd get who she was talking about.

'His favourite place to be. For weeks before Christmas he'd be packing his gear in readiness for coming over the hill. Then he'd have to unpack because he'd need something. For Dad summer *was* Takaka. *Was* this house. *Was* the beach at the end of the lawn. His boat, the fishing, scalloping, barbecues.'

And I'm selling it.

I shouldn't have invited Sash in. I've mostly managed to avoid this since I arrived.

Yet two minutes inside and Sash went for the jugular without even trying. This house was full of wonderful memories of his family that even after all this time he struggled with looking through. Like photos in an album, those memories now flipped over before his eyes. Dad grinning as he held up a nine-kilo snapper. Dad smirking as he tipped his scallop haul out on the lawn. Dad cuddling his daughters in their wet swimsuits. Sash in her bright yellow bikini helping Dad shuck those scallops. Sash backing the big boat into the water.

'The water's boiling.' Sash leaned her butt against the table and crossed her ankles.

Concentrate. He blinked, swallowed, turned away from the understanding and sympathy in those heart-stopping eyes. Banged the pan on an element to cook the bacon; added the spaghetti to the water. Concentrated on cooking. Ignored the old grief threatening to engulf him.

'Are these the colours you've chosen for the

repaint?' Sasha had moved away from the table and now waved some colour swatches in the air.

'I'm going for neutral: Spanish White and Whipped Cream. Should appeal to more punters than if I let my inner being out.' His lungs squeezed out the air they were holding. Sasha had become more beautiful than ever. Her pregnancy made her face glow even while exhaustion dragged her down. Her body was curvier than before, and he itched to hold her, cup her butt in his hands, feel her breasts pressed against his chest.

A soft chuckle brought him to his senses, made him force aside those fanciful pictures as she said, 'I can't imagine painting this room in your favourite rugby team's colours would appeal to many.'

Sasha was grinning at him. And that brought his libido up to speed. Stuck his tongue to the roof of his mouth. Set his nerve endings to tingling. Would it be rude to demand she leave now before he followed through on the need rushing through his body? Knowing he couldn't touch her didn't stop his body reacting in the only way it had ever known.

'Who is your favourite team at the moment, by the way?' she asked in a voice that sounded calm and unaffected. How could that be when he was burning up with need?

'Still the red and blacks. I've followed them from afar.' Another memory flipped over. The ceiling of this room filled with helium balloons, red and black for his team. His mates and their girlfriends hanging around, beers in hand, as the rugby game unfolded that one winter holiday he had ever had here. Their team had won and Dad had handed out more beers and laughed till he'd cried at the whopping score.

Chop, chop. Toss the bacon into the melted butter. So much had gone down during those shocking weeks after Dad had died. So much that he hadn't been able to deal with. Things he'd cruised through by pretending he was handling them well. Making the biggest blunder of his life.

Hiss. Boiling water spilled over the side of the pot. He snatched the lid up, let the bubbling die down. Get a grip, man. Any moment now Sasha was going to charge out of here and call for the paddy wagon to take him away as he was a danger to himself.

You should never have come back. Should've dealt with selling the house from afar.

'Like how? I couldn't do that to Dad. Or me.' Now he'd spoken aloud. Idiot.

A hand touched his arm, fingers pressed firmly. 'You haven't been back since, have you?'

He turned, and instantly regretted it as Sasha's hand fell away. 'Not once.' And up until you walked in here I was handling it.

Her head dipped in acknowledgement. 'Too hard.' Then she moved away, taking her warmth, her scent, across the room. 'Remember the good things, okay?'

'Sure,' he croaked. But that meant remembering the summer of Sasha Wilson. The summer of promise that had turned to dust. Because he'd done the right thing and stood up for his mother and sisters. Elected to support them and walk away from those heady plans of university with Sash.

'Maybe I should go.' She sounded like she was

warring with that idea. Sadness from her eyes ripped him.

What was bothering her so deeply? Not Dad's death, surely? Most likely the consequences. He raised a smile for her because he suddenly did not want to watch her walk out his door. Not yet. 'I'm not eating all this on my own.' He didn't want the quiet of a house empty except for himself and those memories he couldn't face. 'Besides, I haven't told you my plans for tidying up the house over the next month.'

'Guess I'm staying.' Her hand did that maternal thing on her baby belly, rubbing tenderly, her eyes again alight with love and amazement.

His stomach curled in on itself as raw envy crawled up his throat. He wanted that baby to be his. So badly. It was a hunger he hadn't known he had. Until he'd felt that bump when he'd hauled Sasha into his arms for a friendly hug last night. That's when this crazy, mixed-up idea had begun, taking a firmer hold over the day. He wanted to be a dad to Sasha's child. Except the kid already had one. Somewhere.

Her scent warned him moments before her

elbow nudged him out of the way. 'The bacon's beyond crisp.' She lifted the pan, set it on a board to take the heat. 'What's next?' Her eyebrows rose and her mouth lifted on one side.

'Add garlic while I grate Parmesan.'

'Now we're cooking.' She gave him a wink.

'Thanks.' She'd brought him out of his funk with a jab from her elbow and a wink. No one did that for him these days.

The savoury smell of crushed garlic cooking tickled his senses as he broke eggs into a bowl. Adding the cream, he whisked the mixture. And relaxed into the simple pleasure of preparing a meal to share with a—friend.

'This is so good,' Sasha murmured around a mouthful a short while later. 'Where did you learn to cook Italian?'

'As compared to charcoaled sausages on the barbie?' Grady scooped up the last mouthful of sauce from his bowl. 'When I was at med school I started watching cooking shows on TV whenever I needed a break from studying. Something that required no thought from me but was entertaining. After a few weeks I found I'd picked up some clues and began incorporating them in the basic meals I prepared for myself and my flatmates.'

'So you've become a foodie?' She grinned as surprise lightened the green in her eyes to emerald.

'A very amateurish one.' He tried not to stare at her. Hard to do when she looked so radiant after a day of appearing drawn and exhausted. Had he made her feel better? If he'd turned her day around with a simple meal then he was happy.

She told him, 'I've been to Italy twice for the skiing. Tina—she's my friend who got married at the weekend—and I worked in Dubai for two years. We're both ski nuts and Italy in winter was a dream come true, especially in the lake district.'

'Also closer to Dubai than New Zealand.'

'Definitely. Those long-haul flights are hideous. I don't know how Dad does it all the time.'

'He's doing the job he loves.' Grady pushed back his chair. 'Want a coffee?'

'Tea? Coffee at this end of the day tends to wind Flipper up and keep me awake.'

'No tea, sorry.' But it was now at the top of tomorrow's shopping list. 'The next best thing I've got is juice.'

She shook her head, swirling her hair around her face. 'Hot water's fine.' And when he winced, she added, 'Truly. I often drink that at night.'

Her wry smile crunched his heart. 'Who'd have thought? You drinking water at night and me cooking pasta. Have we grown up, or what?'

Sasha stretched her legs out under the table and arched her back, rubbing her lower back with her fingers. Baby protruded further than he'd seen so far. 'Did I mention I've quit skiing for now?' She grinned cheekily and sat up straight again. 'Can you imagine me tearing down the slopes, with Flipper leading the way? I'd end up face first in the snow. So not a good look.'

He should've laughed at the image but he couldn't. Sasha wouldn't have fallen on her face, baby or no baby under her ski suit. She'd always been nimble and surefooted, whether she was dancing, water-skiing, or climbing hills.

What had led him back to this place at the same time as Sasha had come home? She must've been home for visits often over the intervening years.

But it sounded as though she'd returned for good this time. Had he somehow known he'd find her here? Was there a thread of emotion connecting them? 'How long have you been back in the bay?'

Her smile faded, and she straightened up. 'Nearly three months.'

Grady plugged the kettle in. Got out a mug, spooned in instant coffee and sugar. Filled another mug with boiling water. And once again his tongue got the better of him. 'That when you found out you were pregnant?'

'No. That's when I found out Mum had MS.'

Sasha winced as that teaspoon Grady had been gripping clanged in the bottom of the sink. He whipped around to look directly at her, impaling her with his unwavering look. For the second time in twenty-four hours shock stunned him; his face still and his eyes wide. 'Muscular sclerosis? Bloody hell.'

Sasha could understand his shock. It gripped her, too. She'd had no intention of telling him anything about Mum's illness. She hadn't got used to the idea yet. 'Mum and Dad need me here now.' Her breathing was shaky. 'Like your mum and sisters needed you.'

They stared at each other for what felt like an eternity. Then he moved, lifted her from the chair as though she weighed nothing, tucked her against his chest and dropped his chin on top of her head.

She wanted this. Had needed it since the day greaseball had told her where to go with their baby. *That* she'd managed to cope with. But the night Dad had phoned to tell her about Mum she'd believed she must've been a very, very bad person for so much to go wrong. Had she been too selfish in her pursuit of adventure? But her parents had always encouraged her and Jackson to follow their dreams. Should she have stayed in Takaka when she finished school and worked on the orchard? Done some of the hard, heavy work? Would that have saved Mum from getting this horrible disease?

Knowing her self-blame was ridiculous didn't mean she could drop it and feel free of everything. This year seemed to be about life catching up, pay-back for all the fun and antics she'd previously got involved in.

Above her head Grady asked, 'Is Virginia's health the reason Ian's giving up flying internationally?'

'He tells me it is.'

Grady leaned back, pushing his hips against Flipper's hideout as he did. 'You're not sure.'

She'd forgotten how in sync they'd been. How they'd read each other's minds as quickly as thoughts had popped in there. She slipped out of those wonderfully safe arms and sat back down. She might be spilling her guts but she'd do it standing—sitting—tall. 'I'm no doubt overreacting. But Dad is tired all the time and he's lost that joie de vivre that was his trademark.' What if Dad's ill, too?

She'd added to his woes. No father liked to have his daughter turning up on the doorstep pregnant by a man she refused to name or even acknowledge.

After placing the mugs on the table, Grady lifted a chair and spun it round to straddle it. With his arms folded across the top he dropped his chin on them and focused his caring eyes on her. 'Stands to reason he's not sleeping too well. He'll be worried sick about Virginia. I'm only surprised he didn't stop work immediately they found out.'

'Mum wouldn't have a bar of it. Said that she was still capable of running the orchard and looking out for herself. Told Dad if he gave up work it would be like giving in to the MS and undermining her determination to remain as independent as possible for as long as possible.'

'And that's why you're here?'

'Flipper is the perfect excuse.' Though hauling those cases of lemons was getting tougher by the week. Mainly because it worried her she might do some internal damage. She'd become incredibly cautious. 'I suspect Mum sees through me, but I'm giving her the opportunity to let go of things in her own time and fashion. Dad's pleased I'm hanging around. It makes things easier on him to follow Mum's wishes.' Mum and Dad were sorting out a difficult situation by give and take on both sides. Like she and Grady should've done.

'Makes sense.' Grady still watched her with that deep intensity of his.

What did he see? Did her changed persona from wildcat to tame mother-to-be make him glad he'd left her when he had? He'd always enjoyed the fact that she'd had no restraints when it had come to having fun. No way would she put the Cessna into a spin nowadays just for the sheer thrill of twirling round and round as the plane plummeted towards earth.

Grady broke through her reverie. 'Your parents have always been close, even though it seems Ian's spent half their married life flying round the world.'

'Mum reckons that's what made their relationship so special and strong. They haven't had time to learn to take each other for granted.' She picked at the edge of a fingernail. The lime-coloured polish that had matched her wedding outfit looked distinctly jaded. 'I remember them once sharing a single bed when we stayed at my aunt and uncle's. Mum's sister made some smart comment and Mum told her she'd only had half the marriage time Elsie had had and catch-up was always good.'

Grady grinned. 'How old were you when you heard that?'

She chuckled. 'Twelve. The yuk factor was high, believe me. Of course, I wasn't meant to overhear the conversation going on between the sisters.'

She'd learned more than had been good for her at the time. But now? Now she almost envied her parents. Would she ever have the caring, loving, understanding relationship with a man that Mum had?

Her eyes seemed to take on a life of their own, lifting and fixing on Grady, studying him thoroughly for the first time since last night. Until now she'd been too busy pretending he wasn't there to really look for who he'd become.

That slightly long hair was as luxuriant as ever, and not a grey strand in sight. But there were lines on his face that hadn't been there at eighteen. Caused by his father's death? Or working to support his mother and sisters? Dumping her? No, not that. He'd known exactly what he'd been doing that day. His words had been clear, leaving no doubt about his intentions. Blink. Shift focus. Those lips still formed heart-melting smiles. Did they still tease with kisses? Kisses on that sensitive spot behind the ear? Between the breasts? Kisses that devoured her mouth?

'Sash?'

She shot upright, the chair toppling backwards to crash on the tiled floor behind her. What had she been thinking? The problem was she hadn't been thinking. No, Grady was the problem. He'd crept out of his box again. Why couldn't he stay put? Why did he want to upset everything? Throw her off beam? She had begun to get her life back on track. She didn't need this.

So why had she agreed to have a meal with him? Why put herself on the line by walking inside this house, where she'd known nothing but fun and love? Why, why, why?

'Time I went home,' she muttered, and searched around for her keys. Found them in her pocket. Snatched up her jacket and turned for the door.

'Sasha.' Grady caught her arm and turned her gently to face him.

Oh, that gentleness could wipe away a lot of grief—if she let it. It crept in under her skin, under her guard, made her feel again. Feel the love she missed, feel the emptiness waiting to be filled by someone special. Yeah, and set herself up to be left high and dry all over again. No way, sunshine.

She jerked her arm free. 'Thanks for dinner.' She ignored the dismay and hurt in those blue eyes watching her too closely. 'And good luck with all your plans for getting the house ready for the market.'

Not that they'd got around to talking about that. Too busy going over the painful stuff. The front door banged shut behind her, cutting off the light as she stomped down the two steps on her way to the car.

Light flooded the yard. Grady strode out to join her, opening and holding her door while she clambered in. She snapped the ignition to 'on' before looking up into that familiar yet changed face she'd been denying for so long. She locked gazes with Grady, and waited. For what, she had no idea.

For a long moment he didn't move then he leaned forward and she figured he was about to kiss her. Her muscles tensed in anticipation, her hormones did the happy-clappy. Her brain tossed a coin—was this good or bad? When his lips brushed hers she knew it was good. More than good. A girl could get lost in that soft kiss, and when he deepened it, she didn't have a clue about anything but the man kissing her. It was like honey on ice cream, sweet and cool. Delicious. Then his tongue sought hers and cool went to scorching in an instant. So Grady. So them.

Until Flipper got in on the act, delivering a heavy kick to her side. Sasha gasped, rubbed her side.

Grady reared back. He muttered something that sounded like an oath, still staring at her, swallowing hard more than once. Finally he seemed to calm down but kept his distance. 'Where is the baby's father?' He asked so calmly and quietly she wasn't sure she'd heard correctly. But when he added, 'Who is he?' she knew she had.

'He doesn't exist.'

'What?' Grady gaped at her.

'He who doesn't deserve to be acknowledged no longer exists as far as I'm concerned.' Except as greaseball in her head. She looked away. 'He wants no part of my baby's life.' Too much information.

Now he stepped closer, reaching for the ignition to turn it off. Then he peeled her fingers away from the steering-wheel and wrapped her hand in both his. 'The bastard.'

How could two words hold so much anger plus hurt for her, as well as concern and affection?

Lifting her head, she met his gaze. 'The bastard,' she repeated softly. 'He dumped me when the going got tough. Said it had been fun and he'd loved being with me but he didn't love me enough to stay around.'

Grady's hands squeezed tight around hers, loosened. His chest rose sharply. 'Just as I did.'

She said nothing. What was there to say?

'Is that what you think, Sash?'

Gulp. She tugged her hand free, leaned further away from the open door. 'Why wouldn't I?' Shut up, girl. Don't say another thing. Don't show your feelings to this man who stomped on them once already. Don't let him know how worthless he'd made you feel. He used to tell you how strong you were. He wasn't about to find out how untrue that had turned out to be.

'What if he's like me, Sasha?'

Her lips pressed tight, holding back words that had been stewing for years: words she needed to get past. Her hand shook as she reached again for the ignition.

'What if he's lying? What if he does want you and comes back one day?'

Her hand banged down on her knee. Her chin shot out and she fixed him with a glare. Anger, pain, despair all combined to roll up her throat and spill out between them. 'He's worse. He's dumped his baby daughter. He doesn't want to be a part of her life.' She reached out to grab the front of his shirt and shake him. 'That makes me the worst mother possible because my girl won't ever know her father. I didn't plan on getting pregnant but I still thought I was with a man who cared for me, who would care for his child.' She wouldn't have had a relationship with him otherwise. 'I made a bad choice.'

She refused to think about the implications of Grady's revelation. That he might want to come back for her. It wasn't possible. And even if he did it wasn't going to happen. She was done with risking her heart.

Grady placed his hands on her shoulders. 'We all make mistakes, Sasha. But please stop thinking your baby's mother is bad. You are so special. She'll never want for love or kindness. You have those in bucketloads. You love her so much already it's amazing to see. When you touch your tummy your eyes go all misty with it.' His Adam's apple bobbed. 'She's a very lucky little girl.'

Talk about knocking her for six. Never would she have imagined Grady saying something so heart-warming, so caring. 'Thank you' was the best she could manage around the tears clogging her throat. She reached up to place her hand on his cheek. 'I needed to hear that.'

His eyes locked with hers. So much emotion streamed out at her. Too many emotions to read. 'If you did then I'm glad I told you.'

Her stomach hurt from clenching. Her head throbbed from holding in the tears. Her heart ached—because in a different world, at a different time, Grady would've been the perfect man for her.

She turned away. 'I'd better go home and get some shut-eye. I seem to need more of that these days.'

As he began closing her door he whispered, 'Goodnight, Sasha. Sleep tight.'

CHAPTER SIX

'SLEEP TIGHT. LIKE HOW?' Sasha asked into the dark for the umpteenth time as she slapped her pillow into shape. Dropping her head back down, the air whooshed out of her lungs. 'Any sleep at all would be good.'

Flipper gave her a wee nudge.

'You need to sleep, too, sweetheart. Swimming's over for the day.' Sasha ran her hands over her stomach, revelling in the tightness of her skin and the life under her palms. This pregnancy might've been unplanned but it had turned out to be the most exciting and life-changing thing to happen.

Don't forget the most worrying. Not that being pregnant was troubling, but what came afterwards was. Being a full-time mother, making all the decisions regarding her daughter and praying she got them right. There was no one to fall back on when she needed reassurance. Once she'd have had her parents but really they now had too much to deal with to need their daughter demanding help with a problem she'd caused. No, she was on her own for this ride.

Nothing in her life had undermined her confidence as pregnancy had. The stack of books on the bedside table about caring for a baby underscored that. The contents list on her internet screen highlighted that. She soaked up all the available information, ignored her colleagues' comments that nurses worried too much, and read some more.

'I've totally confused myself. For every expert who says do one thing there are as many saying the opposite.'

'You'll be fine,' Jess kept telling her. 'The moment I place your baby in your arms it will all come together. Believe me. I felt the same before Nicholas was born.'

Which did nothing to bolster her confidence. It wasn't as though she could go bang on the doors of the experts who got it wrong and give them a telling-off. She didn't know who was right or who was wrong.

She sighed. 'Grady's shown up and all these unwanted needs are ramping up inside me.' Another sigh, softer this time. 'He kissed me goodnight.' Her finger traced her lips. Never in all the intervening years had it occurred to her she'd receive another Grady kiss. She should've rammed the car in reverse and shot out of his yard faster than a 747 on take-off. But she hadn't. Because? That kiss had sneaked up on her. It had been wonderful. Exciting, caring, hot. Grady. *Did he regret leaving me?*

He'd said something about wanting to come back. To her. That didn't make sense when he was planning to sell the house. Had he been testing the waters? Or had he been consumed with the need to taste her, to find he'd done the right thing when he'd left her?

Her fists banged down on the mattress. 'Go away, Grady. Take your kiss with you. Climb back in your box and leave me alone. Please.'

'Please,' she whispered again. Deep breaths. In,

out. In, out. Relax. Arms first. Fingers uncurled, hands loose, lower arms. Upper arms. Toes.

The urge to roll on her side and face the empty half of her big bed was relentless. Refusing to give in, she stared at the ceiling, her hands clenched at her sides, and breathed deeply. Uncurled her fingers, shook her hands loose.

Imagined Grady in that space next to her. His long legs reaching to the bottom of the bed. His wide chest covering more than his share of the mattress. His head sunk into the pillow beside her. If she rolled over she could move into the warmth of those strong arms he'd placed around her earlier. His hands could splay across her back, holding her safe. That beautiful mouth on her skin. Tonguing her into a frenzy.

She rolled sideways, her hand reaching across the gap to touch—cold, harsh reality. That side of the bed was empty. Chilly. No warm, male body. No Grady.

Grady was not real to her any more. Really? He was hardly an overactive figment of her imagination. Those hands that had held her shoulders earlier had been warm and strong and real. That mouth that had smiled and grinned and grimaced and kissed her had been real.

Her eyes filled, the tears burst over her eyelids, flooded her face, her pillow, her dreams. 'Real or not, I can't give you my heart again, Grady.'

Grady finally went back into his box.

Every muscle in Sasha's body complained of fatigue, as it had all day long. If she didn't get some decent, deep sleep tonight she'd be toast tomorrow. If this was what a couple of less-than-perfect nights did to her then once Flipper arrived she'd be hopeless. Until now she'd never had trouble sleeping.

'That's because I always exhausted myself physically throughout the day. Can't do that at the moment. And if I turn up at work overtired too often, Mike and Rory are going start asking questions about my ability to do the job.' Fear bounced down her spine. This job was very important. Without it she'd have to leave the bay and head to Nelson. Away from her mother at a time she needed to be here. That made her feel cold just thinking about it. 'So I have to sleep a full eight hours tonight. No argument.'

Rubbing her aching back, she reached for her medical bag and headed up the mud- and rock-strewn driveway to Campbell McRae's bungalow. Behind the outbuildings the high peaks of the Wakamarama Range sent chilly shadows over the surrounding paddocks, keeping the ground damp and cold. Hopefully, at this time of the year trampers weren't walking the Heaphy Track. Too easy to slip over on the muddy track and suffer serious injuries.

The bungalow's front door swung open as she stepped carefully onto the uneven veranda. Bracing for her next call, she smiled. 'Hi, Sadie.'

'Hello, Sasha. Campbell's in a right old snot today.' The middle-aged, squat woman scowled. 'He thinks we should all be at his beck and call.'

Sasha wiped her shoes on the not-so-clean doormat. 'What's bothering him?'

'Just about everything you care to think of.' Sadie had the fortitude of a saint. Her brother's situation made him very bad-tempered, which was completely understandable, but not nice.

'Have you been changing the dressings like I showed you?' Campbell's leg had been amputated above the knee four weeks ago due to complications with his diabetes.

'When he lets me near him.' Sadie slammed the door shut. 'He's in the lounge.'

Sasha headed down the narrow, dark hallway, trying hard not to trip over any of the myriad objects lying on the floor. 'Afternoon, Campbell.' She'd learned right from her first visit not to say good afternoon as Campbell would instantly dispute the good component.

'You're late. I've been waiting for ages.' The forty-four-year-old grizzled from where he sat by the grubby window, his crutches lying nearby. 'You parked in the wrong place. I've told you about that before. One day that goat's going to run its horns down the side of that fancy wagon of yours and then you'll come complaining to me.'

She'd forgotten about the goat. Blame her jaded brain on a certain man back in Takaka. He'd been following her around in her head all day. 'How's that leg been? Are you doing those lifting exer-cises I showed you?'

'A fat lot of good they do. It's not like I'm going to be out running around after the stock, is it?'

In other words, no. Sasha explained what she'd explained often. 'You need to keep those thigh muscles moving. You want them strong for when you're fitted with your prosthetic leg.'

Campbell had the grace to look a tiny bit sorry. 'I know you're right, but I don't see the point. Wearing a tin leg won't make it any easier to get around the farm. I can drive the tractor but how do I get on it in the first place? Huh?'

She recognised the self-pity for what it was, and didn't blame him. Who would be happy in his situation? A lot of self-doubt as well as fear went on in an amputee's mind until they accepted their new way of life. Leaning down to remove the dressing from his stump, she asked, 'Have you thought about buying a four-wheeled farm bike? More manoeuvrable and lower to the ground than a tractor.'

'Do you know how much those things cost? I'm no millionaire.'

'You might be able to find a second-hand one. Go on line and see what's around.' Did he have a computer?

'Go on line? That's the modern answer to everything.'

'Yes, it is, and it's not going to change any time soon.' Sasha smiled at him, refusing to let his mood affect her. Carefully touching the wound with glove-covered fingers, she was pleased to see last week's redness and puffiness had gone. 'This is healing nicely. That infection's improved.'

Grunt. 'Jessica stood over me until I swallowed those bullets she calls pills. She's bossier than you.'

Good for you, Jess. Her friend had covered her rounds while she'd been in Christchurch. Sasha cleaned the stump and placed a new dressing over it. 'Okay, Campbell, show me those exercises. I want to see you do them twice before I go.'

Campbell looked away. 'I'm too sore.'

Sasha crossed to a chair, removed the magazines and knitting to sit down. 'I'm not going anywhere.'

Her patient glared at her. 'Anyone ever tell you you're stubborn?'

'All my patients.' She continued smiling, but she was worried. Campbell appeared more belligerent than usual. 'Is something other than your leg bothering you, Campbell?'

His mouth tightened as he stared out the window. 'I've lived here since I was a nipper. Don't know any other way of life.'

'It's the same for Sadie.'

'Yeah, but she can leave any time she likes. Nothing to keep her here.'

A man's man now reduced to hobbling around on crutches. Eventually he'd be able to walk again but he'd never be chasing up the hills and through the valleys with his working dogs the way he used to.

'I'd say Sadie has the same reasons for staying as you. Family, history, the comfort of knowing this place and the land.' Those things had brought *her* back home when the going had got tough. Was she saying the right things? Should she shut up and go back to the medical centre, get Mike to arrange an appointment for Campbell with a counsellor that he'd never keep?

'You reckon?' His belligerence backed off a little. Then he shifted his butt and, gripping the armrest, lifted his thigh off the chair. Put it down. Lifted it again. His face contorted with the effort. 'Weak as a kitten,' he said, self-disgust clear in his voice.

Sasha stood up and crossed over to him. 'What's that wrapper you've stuffed under your backside?'

Campbell's thigh dropped to the chair and stayed there. 'Chocolate.'

'I'll check your glucose level before I go.' She wanted to shake him, tell him he was putting his life in jeopardy, but he knew that better than her. He was already dealing with the consequences of not watching his diet carefully, of having allowed his diabetes go uncontrolled because he'd refused to accept it existed.

Shock rippled down her spine. Was that what she was doing with Grady? Not accepting that they were different now? That they had matured and learned a lot about living? She certainly hadn't forgiven him. Was she meant to? Might help if she did. Might wipe out some of the hurt and anger that had resurfaced in the last two days. Might stop the need for him that crawled through her body, warmed her blood and started an ache in her sex whenever he was near.

'It's twelve point one.'

'What?'

'My glucose,' Campbell grumbled.

'Let's double-check that.' She wouldn't put it past Campbell to have grabbed any figure out of the air.

Two house calls and one hundred and fifty kilometres later Sasha sped into the parking area behind the medical centre and leapt out of her vehicle.

'Please, Flipper, please, please, kick me. Hard as you like. Bruise my ribs. I don't care. I need to know you're okay.' Please.

She skidded on the mat at the back door, righted herself and raced down the hall towards the nurses' room. 'Jess, where are you?' She spilled into the room and ran slap bang into Grady.

Strong hands gripped her shoulders, held her upright. 'Hey, slow down. What's up?'

'Where's Jess?' She wriggled out of his hold and peered behind him, looking for her midwife. 'Jess, I can't feel Flipper moving. She hasn't kicked for hours. Is she all right? Tell me I'm being silly, that she's fine. Jess?'

'Anything out of the ordinary happen today?' Jessica stood up from the desk and came straight to her, reached for her hand at the same moment Grady caught her shoulders again, this time from behind.

'I—I picked up J-Josh T-Templeton for a cuddle and my back t-tweaked.' Why had she bent down to lift the overweight toddler? *Because he's so cute and he was holding his arms up, begging for a hug.* 'Have I hurt my b-baby?' She'd never lift another child, another thing, until after her baby girl was born. She'd sit in a chair and read a book twenty-four seven. Promise. *Just be okay, baby.*

Jess squeezed her hand. 'Deep breaths, Sasha. How long exactly since you last felt her move?'

'I don't want to breathe. I want to feel my baby moving.'

'Sasha, how long?' Grady echoed Jess's question. Those strong fingers on her shoulders began making soothing circular movements.

She didn't want to be soothed. She wanted Flipper kicking as though her life depended on it. She'd take all the pounding she could get to know her baby was safe, and only taking a longer than usual rest. 'Jess, Grady, do something.'

Her knees buckled under her. Grady caught her, held her tight, backed her against his chest. She tried to soak up his strength but it wasn't enough. It didn't answer the overriding question. Was her baby all right? Was she alive?

'Easy, Sasha. I'll examine you immediately but there's probably nothing to worry about.' His tone was soothing but that didn't help either.

Grady was going to examine her? Not in a million years. That would be too weird.

This isn't about you. Or Grady. Your baby's life is all that matters. Who examines you is irrelevant as long as they know what they're doing.

Jessica glared at Grady. 'You're overriding my position?'

Sasha pulled out of Grady's arms, her hands holding her belly. Waiting for a movement, imagining one and knowing she was wrong. Wanting didn't mean getting. She looked from Jess to Grady.

'We'll examine Sasha.'

Something in his eyes must've made Jess feel okay with that because she backed off immediately and gave Sasha a loving smile. 'Let me help you up on the bed.'

But before she could dredge up any kind of answer Grady had taken her arm to lead her across the room. She wanted to relax in against Grady's body and feel safe. But she couldn't. Not when Flipper needed all her focus. Flipper. 'Oh, no.' A chill sliced through her, lifted bumps on her skin. 'Last night I told Flipper to stop swimming and go to sleep. This is my fault,' she wailed. Where had that primal sound come from? Had she made it? Her bottom lip trembled so badly she had to bite down hard.

'No, Sasha, this is not your fault. Babies do

this. Chances are your little girl is absolutely fine.' He spoke evenly, quietly. Professionally. He was being a doctor, no more, no less.

That calmed her somewhat, helped her take that breath Jess wanted, got her brain working so she could answer the question she hadn't got to yet. 'I'm not sure of the last time I felt her move. I think I might've while I was with Campbell McRae.' Her lip trembled again. 'But I can't be a hundred per cent sure.'

'Was that your last call?' Grady's hand under her elbow gave her balance as she climbed onto the bed, feeling more than ever like a heavily pregnant hippopotamus.

'I did two more, and then had to drive back from Paton's Rock,' she answered.

'So a couple of hours all up.' Jess stood on the other side of the bed. 'The usual thing to do now is make you lie down for one or two hours and relax—'

'Relax?' she shrieked. 'When I haven't felt anything from my baby all that time? I don't think so.'

Jess's calm smile didn't help a bit. 'Let me finish. You've been racing around all day, visiting patients, right?'

Sasha pursed her lips and glared at her friend. 'So?'

'So when you're busy you won't always notice baby's movements as much as when you're taking it easy. Lie back, Sasha, place your hands on your tummy and wait quietly.'

'Since when have I ever done quietly?' she grumbled, but lay back on the pillows.

'Since you left that loser and came home,' Jessica told her.

My own fault for asking. Jess had never hidden the truth, at least not about greaseball whom she'd never met but had an opinion about anyway. 'Thanks, pal.'

'You're welcome.' Jess gave her a big smile. 'Now, relax, will you?'

Beside her Grady lifted her wrist, pressed his fingers onto her radial artery. She watched his lips moving as he counted her pulse. His eyes had become inscrutable. Because of that loser comment? This was probably as strange a situation for Grady as it was for her. But if she could handle it then so could he. Only the baby mattered. Not his bruised ego or hers. Despite last night's conversation about the past they were trying to be friends, and this was a good way to start. Don't think about the kiss.

'Pulse is normal.' He laid her wrist down as though it was made of the finest crystal.

'Why did you even take it? I wouldn't have thought it necessary.'

'Gives me something to do.' He gave a deprecating smile. 'Jessica's got everything covered.'

'What about listening in? Flipper might have something to say.'

'Why not? Can't do any harm.' Friendliness had taken over his gaze.

But when Sasha tugged her top up, exposing her rounded belly for all to see, it was Grady's bobbing Adam's apple that caught her attention. So he was having massive trouble with the situation. She shouldn't have suggested he do this bit. Should've asked Jess.

She turned in entreaty to Jess. Her friend nodded once in understanding and shoved the earpieces in her ears before placing the cold bell on her abdomen.

Sasha crossed her fingers and held her breath, and bit down on that quivering lip again. Please, please, please, please…

She watched Jess closely, looking for any change in her eyes or mouth, her expression. She knew Jess well, had learned to read her over the months as their friendship had deepened. But she saw nothing. Panic roared up her throat. She bit down hard to block off a cry. Her hands turned into fists and she thumped the bed at her sides.

'Shh.' Grady's hand covered one of hers. 'You're making it hard for Jessica to hear anything.'

She shifted her stare from Jess to Grady, locked eyes with him. Saw nothing but concern and caring, not fear and worry. *Masking the Truth from Your Patient 101?*

'I hear a heartbeat.' Jess gave her a tense smile. 'Grady?' She handed him the stethoscope and picked up Sasha's other hand. 'That's good, Sasha. The relaxing will help—if you ever get around to following my instructions.'

Grady still held her gaze, having reached blindly for the stethoscope, and now she saw a crack in his demeanour. Relief? Worry? Love? No, couldn't be that. Had to be the anxiety one friend naturally felt for another in this predicament. She had Jess and her parents with her on this journey but she also knew whatever Grady was feeling she had him with her too, at least until Flipper was born. Some of the chill racking her loosened.

He asked, 'Do you mind if I listen, Sasha?'

'Go for it. What does it mean if you can hear the heartbeat but she's not moving?' All her nursing training had gone out the door. She was like any other mother, totally freaked out and needing answers that she knew they probably couldn't give.

Grady placed the bell on her abdomen. She stared at him now, watching, waiting for any reaction. He was as good as Jess. Nothing showed.

Okay, guys, you're my friends. Help me out here. What's happening with my baby girl?

Sweat popped on her brow, her palms, thighs, between her toes. She wouldn't think of those questions that had no answers. She wouldn't. She wouldn't. 'Grady? Talk to me.'

At least his fingers weren't shaking as he handed the stethoscope to Jess. 'I don't want you panicking...' His eyebrows rose and his mouth curved upward ever so slightly. 'Okay, no more than you already are. Yes, there's a heartbeat and I'm sure everything is all right. The suggestion of relaxing and waiting is fine if you're living close to a hospital. But since you're two hours away from the nearest one I think as a precaution a cardiotocograph might be appropriate. It's normal in these situations, Sash. Isn't it, Jessica?'

'Absolutely.' Jess looked at her all funny like. As though she was about to cry. 'I'm going to phone the hospital in Nelson right now.'

Sasha sat up, gripping Jess's hand so hard she probably cracked some bones. 'What aren't you telling me? Why are you trying not to cry? What's wrong with my baby?'

Jess gasped, but didn't pull her hand free. Probably couldn't because of her vice-like grip. 'I think everything's A-okay in there. But I do want you checked out so we can be absolutely sure.' A tear tracked down her cheek. 'Sasha, you're my bestest friend and you're pregnant. More than you can believe, I want this going right for you. You deserve it. You're so brave and strong and big-hearted. The man who gave you this gift already dealt you one bad card. You don't deserve any more.'

Sasha couldn't talk for the tears clogging her throat. Instead, she broke a few more bones in Jess's hand.

On her other side Grady cleared his throat. 'We'll head off very shortly. Jessica can text us about the appointment when she's spoken to the hospital. You also need to tell Ian and Virginia we won't be there for dinner. And why.'

'Mum and Dad.' Glad someone was thinking straight. 'They'll be beside themselves if I tell them what's happening.'

Grady parked his backside on the edge of the bed. 'Let me talk to them. I can reassure them and promise to phone the moment you've been checked over. But you can't avoid telling them. They should know.'

'It will stress them out.' They should hear it

from her, not Grady. Especially not from Grady.
But she was in a hurry. She had to get to Nelson a.s.a.p. She had to know what was going on
in her tummy. Had to know her baby girl really
was fine. She nodded, totally at a loss for words.

Jess was already at her desk punching in numbers she seemed to know off by heart. That had to
be a good sign, didn't it? This happened so often
it was routine. She hadn't heard of an excess of
distressed babies being born in Golden Bay.

Then another urgent need caught her. 'I'll be a
minute. Then we're out of here.'

When Grady lifted one eyebrow she flushed
pink. 'Bathroom.'

His grin was as unexpected as it was fun.
'Babies and bladders, eh? A tricky combination,
I'm told.'

A whisper of something rippled through her
that had nothing to do with the fear gripping her
so tight her muscles felt on the verge of tearing.

I could fall in love with this man all over again.

But right now she didn't have the time or energy. All that was for her baby.

CHAPTER SEVEN

ONCE THEY REACHED the far side of Takaka Hill Grady drove quickly. He still kept an alert eye on the road. The icy conditions of two nights ago had improved to the point that there was little to worry about, but there was no escaping the fact that midwinter reigned and the temperature hovered not much above zero. But he desperately wanted to be at Nelson Hospital and hear someone telling Sasha her baby was fine.

Sasha was too quiet. For her own good. For his heart rate. From what he'd heard through that stethoscope he was satisfied the baby would be all right. It's what he'd have told any patient in the same situation if they'd presented at his clinic, and felt comfortable about it. But this was Sash. So different. So much a part of him. Sash.

He knew she was hurting. The fear lunged out of those green orbs to lance his heart every time she looked at him, which was less and less the further they got from the medical centre. There were dents below her bottom lip from those teeth. She'd broken through the skin in one spot.

Worse, for him anyway, as there was nothing he could do to make her feel any better than what he was already doing. Never had he felt so helpless. In this situation being a doctor hadn't helped one iota. Remaining neutral was impossible.

At least she hadn't argued when he'd said he was driving her across. When he'd spoken to Ian the man had sounded relieved he was going with Sasha. Good to know her father wasn't averse to him being on the scene. There'd been a shade of panic and fear in Ian's voice. He'd hated not being able to totally dispel that. Nothing but the cardiotocograph results would. Favourable results.

Reaching over, he lifted one of Sasha's cold hands in his and rubbed his thumb back and forth over across it. Shivers kept her hand in constant motion. 'Have you thought of real names for your baby yet?'

Slowly she turned to face him. The bewitching green shade of her eyes had dulled and that hit him hard. His stomach sucked in on itself. Pain knotted in the base of his gut. He should be able to allay her fears, take the hurt for her, but he couldn't. Firstly, nothing on earth could make a mother feel unfazed in this situation. And then, well, this baby had nothing to do with him, no matter how much he wanted it to. Like him last night, Jessica had called the father a bastard. No matter what the circumstances, the man had had no right to desert Sasha and their baby so completely.

Just as well I don't know who he is.

'Why?' Sasha whispered.

Why what? What had he asked? Names. 'Just thinking that Flipper could possibly stick even after she's born if you keep calling her that.'

'You weren't thinking Flipper would look wrong on the headstone if—if…?' Tears diluted her words, her tone, making her sound completely lost. Which she was.

Risking Sash's wrath, he pulled over to the side of the road and turned to pull her into his arms. His hands spread across her back to rub as gently as he could. 'Sash, sweetheart, I promise I was not thinking that at all.' I was trying to divert your thoughts for a very brief moment, only I appear to have made them worse. 'Flipper's going to be fine.' He held off promising. Not only was that going too far without back-up knowledge, it tempted the devil.

'Melanie. That's what I'm calling her.'

'Your grandmother's name?'

'Yes.'

'I like it. Melanie Wilson.' Melanie O'Neil. Worked for him.

She rubbed her face back and forth across the front of his jacket, sniffing and crying. It wrenched his heart. Sash didn't do crying. Okay, she didn't use to. Pending motherhood had changed her. In lots of ways. His arms tightened further around her in the useless hope he could absorb some of her pain and fear. Never had he felt so utterly useless. So unable to do something positive for someone he loved.

'Can we go now?'

At least, that's what he thought her muffled words were. 'Sure.' Afraid of her reaction and yet needing to do it, he dropped a light kiss on the top of her head before straightening up. Then he concentrated on getting his precious cargo to Nelson.

There was so much more he wanted to give her in the future, but that was a slow trip, remember? He couldn't rush her, and certainly not at this moment.

Sasha gripped Grady's hand as they walked heavily towards the clinic the night-time receptionist directed them to. She'd been doing a lot of handholding since she'd barged back into work as fear overwhelmed her, beat her down. What had happened to her? She used to stand tall, hide all her emotions behind a fixed smile and a smart-assed comment.

Since the advent of Flipper she was an emotional cot case, and totally unable to hide it. 'Will you come in with me?' Talk about asking too much of him, but at this moment, with her heart pounding so hard her ears hurt, she'd have asked the first person she came across if she hadn't got Grady with her.

'Try and keep me away.'

'Good answer.' She tried to smile at him, she really did, but all she managed was a lopsided mouth and an eyeful of tears.

'Hey, hang in there, Sash. Won't be long now before we know what Flipper's up to.'

For the first time she was happy to hear him call her Sash. Now it didn't sound so much sexy as loving. And caring. And right. 'That's what frightens me. There's a huge what-if clanging around my skull that I'm refusing to answer.' Her baby girl had to be all right. Had to be. Was all this squeezing in her gut doing the baby any good? No matter how hard she tried, she couldn't stop the waves of panic gripping and tensing every muscle in her body.

'Here we are.' Grady marched them up to the desk. 'Sasha Wilson for a CTG.'

The guy sitting behind the counter stood up immediately. 'Hi, Sasha, I'm Glen. I've been waiting for you. How was your trip over the hill?'

She didn't have a clue. Apart from that moment when Grady had stopped to hug her she'd been totally unaware of anything apart from her baby. But the guy was trying to be friendly and put her at ease. 'Great.'

'If you go through that door over on the left you'll find a gown to slip into. Leave only your underwear on. There's another door leading out of the cubicle into our room. I'll meet you there.'

She nodded. 'Thank you. Um, can Grady come with me?'

'Of course. Fathers are always welcome.'

'Father?' If only. But it wasn't surprising Glen had made that mistake. Grady was stepping up like an anxious father. She'd have to think about what that meant later. When, if, life ever got back to normal.

Glen turned a deep red and spluttered, 'And friends. It's best you have someone with you.'

In case you find something very wrong. Sasha's bottom lip stung sharply as her teeth dug in again. Running, she reached the door leading into the cubicle and slammed it shut behind her.

'Please, baby girl, please, make your heart go bang, bang, bang for the man.'

Her trousers hit the floor, followed by her jacket, blouse and thermal top. Goose-bumps covered her as the cold air touched her warm skin. The gown she wrapped around herself was thin and inadequate for winter temperatures. *Who cares?*

'Please, Melanie, be all right. We've got so much ahead of us. There're many things I want to show you, teach you, give you.'

Ahh. She stuffed a fist in her mouth to stifle the scream pouring over her tongue. Melanie. Since when had she used the baby's proper name? Since she'd become fearful for her safety. Did this mean—? No. No. No. It must not.

'Sash?' The door opened a crack and Grady asked, 'Are you ready?'

Sniff. *That depends. I'll never be ready if the news is bad.* Dropping her fist to her side, she slipped through the doorway and headed to where Glen waited.

Of course Grady picked up her hand and gave her a squeeze. 'Let's do it, shall we?'

'First we'll check the foetal heart rate.' Glen explained everything.

Sasha's gaze was glued to Glen, watching for every nuance in his expression. Finally she got a thumbs-up. 'Here, look at this. It's all good. Baby's fine.' He tore off a printout from the machine reading the baby's heart rate and handed it to her. Grady's head was touching hers as they stared at the lines in front of them.

Splish, splash. Drops of moisture hit the back of her hands. Her shoulders dropped forward as she curled over her precious baby. 'Oh, Flipper, you're okay, baby. Thank goodness. I don't know what I'd have done if you hadn't been.'

Grady wrapped those strong, safe arms around her and his chin bumped the top of her head. Above her she heard a sniff. 'Grady?' She pulled back just enough to see his face and the tears tracking down his cheeks.

'I'm so glad for you, Sasha.'

Cupping his cheek with one hand, she whispered, 'Thank you. For everything. I needed you here with me.'

Some time later, though probably only a couple of minutes, Glen cleared his throat and said, 'I'd like to take you for an ultrasound so we can make sure that the placenta is functioning properly and check the transfer of blood and oxygen through the cord to baby.'

'So we're not in the clear yet.' Her smile faded.

'Everything's fine. It's just precautionary. Since you're here we might as well make the most of your trip.' Glen handed her another copy of the printout. 'For your baby album.'

Though her fingers shook as she took it, she felt the awful weight of fear finally lift. *For her baby album.* How normal did that sound?

Grady wound the car slowly and carefully around the hairpin bends on Takaka Hill, determined not to wake Sasha until he reached her cottage. She had exited that hospital quietly, happily and utterly exhausted.

The news had been all good. Sasha had phoned Jessica and then her parents. Everyone would sleep well tonight, though none as well as the woman beside him.

They'd eaten fish and chips parked outside the takeaway shop in Nelson. Make that he'd devoured more than his share while Sasha had pecked at a piece of crispy batter-covered blue cod and a couple of chips. Then she'd fallen sound asleep, curled into the corner made by her seat and the front door.

After clicking her seat belt in place and tossing into the rubbish bin the paper that had wrapped their meal, he'd headed for home. Home. Something tight and warm settled under his ribs. He'd been searching for a place to call that ever since he'd left Sasha.

Returning to Nelson from Golden Bay that day eleven years ago to go and see the transport company's boss and make arrangements for taking over Dad's contract had been hard. With every kilometre he'd driven he'd felt his heart being torn further from his chest, pulled by the girl he'd left behind, yanked by his mother's needs in Nelson.

He'd never regretted changing his plans of going to university in order to support Mum and the girls. It's what any man worthy of being called that would do—step up for his family. The price had been high, though. Sash. He might've grown up in Nelson but it hadn't felt like home since that day.

He'd known only despair. A week earlier his father had gone for ever. That day Sasha had gone, forced out of his life by him. Gone. For ever, if that heart-tearing, gut-slicing look in her eyes as the truth had dropped home in her mind had been anything to go by.

In reality, Golden Bay had never been home for him either, just the place he'd gone with his family for the most amazing, carefree summer holidays—and Sash.

Now, from the moment he'd set eyes on her at the accident scene, that word had been creeping into his vocabulary on a regular basis. Already he'd changed his mind about what colour to paint the inside of his house from those bland, neutral shades. Earlier in the day he'd phoned through an order for paint a shade of terracotta that made him feel happy and warm. He'd also called on the local plumber for bathroom brochures, to see what they had on offer.

You're setting yourself up for the biggest fall. Just because it's starting to feel like home in Golden Bay it doesn't mean Sash will want a bar of you in any other way than as friends.

He also didn't have a job to keep food in the pantry and petrol in the tank.

The shuffle of Sasha's jacket had his eyes flicking sideways. Her hand circled her belly. In the almost-dark of the car's interior he couldn't see if she had woken.

'Sash?' he whispered, as he focused back on the road.

Nothing. So even in sleep she was conscious of her baby. He liked that.

Finally, nearly two hours after they'd set out from Nelson he turned into Sasha's drive and cut the motor. Now what? Sasha was sleeping the sleep of emotional exhaustion. He so did not want to wake her. But he couldn't go scrabbling around in that massive bag of hers for keys to the house. He couldn't take her to his place with only one bed.

Now, there's a thought. Down, boy. Hard not to react to Sash when she dominated his mind all the time, tormented his body. Go find a way into the cottage and put those thoughts of hot sex on the back burner.

The house key sat under the potted lemon tree on the top step. 'Nice one, Sash.'

With the door open and lights on, Grady returned to Sasha. Opening the door carefully so as not to dump her on the drive, he scooped her into his arms and headed inside, pushing the door shut behind them with his butt.

Now that the panic of hours earlier had gone he allowed himself to breathe in the sweet scent of Sash. Honeysuckle. Reminding him of summer days and nights. Anything to do with Sash reminded him of hot summer days and hotter nights. Tightened his gut with longing. Sent waves of heat through his body, all aiming for his sex. Her warm body tucked against his chest did nothing to halt these waves of desire cascading over him. His body had missed hers. Had longed to plunge deep inside her, to feel her heat surround him, to know her passion as she shattered in his arms.

Great one, O'Neil. Just what the doctor ordered. A full-blown hard-on. One that would have no release. Sasha wasn't his. Hadn't been in ages, and wasn't about to become so. She carried another man's baby. It didn't matter that the man had left her high and dry.

Yeah, and you still lust after her. Still love her.

Yeah, and I can't do a thing about that.

What happened to trying to woo her back slowly?

I just ran out of patience. And, I suspect, opportunity—if I ever had that. Sasha had made it very plain she wasn't interested in a rerun of their previous relationship. What about a newer version? A grown-up, take-all-life's-punches relationship? She wasn't interested in that either. She might be saying her baby's father was a bastard but there'd been a ton of hurt in her voice, indicating she might still be in love with the guy.

Ignoring his painfully squeezing heart, Grady turned into her bedroom and nudged the light switch with an elbow. The big bed beckoned. It would be so easy to lie down with Sash and hold her close as she slept. If she woke he'd have to rethink that because he doubted he'd be able to keep his hands off her. Patience had always been his middle name—until he'd returned to Golden Bay and seen this woman currently in his arms and drooping in all directions as though she was boneless.

Yet the moment she woke she'd remember all that fear brought on by her baby's silence and those muscles would tighten up.

And he still had a boner to contend with. Seemed a dose of cold, hard reality hadn't quietened that down. Best put her to bed. Don't go there, he warned his southern brain. Behave.

Sash stirred as he placed her on the bed. When he tucked the sheet and quilt up to her chin she blinked her eyes open. 'Grady?' she croaked.

'Shh. Go back to sleep, Sash.'

Her eyes opened wider. 'Why are you putting me to bed?'

'Because it's late and you were sound asleep in my car.' He stepped back from that tempting picture of sweetness. Run, man, while you still can. Because whatever you want, Sash will hate you tomorrow if you take advantage of her right now.

But Sash wasn't thinking straight. Her hand slid out from under the covers and grabbed at his shirt. 'Grady.' She tugged him. When he didn't budge she pushed up the bed and leaned closer.

'Thank you for today. For being there. For being you. I needed all of that.'

Another tug, and this time he didn't resist. Couldn't resist. Those lips were smiling, those eyes drawing him in, that honeysuckle tickling his sensory receptors. He bent down, wrapped his arms around her and pulled her up close so that he could feel against him the length of the body he craved in the deep of the night.

Sash twisted her head so that her lips locked on his. Finally, finally he tasted her. When her tongue slipped into his mouth he knew he'd found his Sash. And yet this was not his Sash. A different woman, confident in a less brash way. Gentled by her baby? By circumstances? Then her hands gripped his biceps and her swollen breasts pushed into his chest and he forgot to think. Just savoured the moment, the bone-melting kiss. He was home.

Lifting his hands to her head, his fingers combed into her silky hair. So soft. In response she pressed her hips forward. Rubbed up against his obvious need for her.

And reminded him with her baby bump why

he shouldn't be doing this. Dropping his hands to her shoulders, he separated their bodies, put air between them. Let go his hold. Stepped back further. 'Sash.' Swallow. 'Sasha, I'm sorry.'

Her butt abruptly landed on the edge of the bed, as though her legs couldn't hold her up without any assistance from him. The ring-covered fingers of her left hand pressed into her lips. Surprise glittered out of her eyes. 'You're sorry?' she asked around those fingers. 'Then so am I.' Taking her hand away, she stared up at him. 'Grady, I shouldn't have kissed you. It was obvious you were moving away from me and in my sleep-hazed state I had to follow.'

Hit me in the gut, why don't you? 'I understand. It's okay.' Lying was all right sometimes, wasn't it? For sure, he wasn't about to lay his heart in those trembling hands twisting in her lap. She wasn't ready for that. She might never want him again, despite that kiss. He'd still have to try, but not this way. Slowly, slowly. In other words, be patient.

'I need to get into bed now. Properly.'

'Of course. Do you want a hot drink once you're sorted?'

'Is hot chocolate on the menu?' Her smile was shy and sliced right in deep, twisting through his heart.

'Coming right up,' he gasped, and turned abruptly for the door and the chill of the other rooms. Her bedroom had become hotter than an inferno. To the point he half expected to melt into a puddle of need at her feet.

In the pokey kitchen he banged cupboard doors as he looked for a mug, some chocolate and sugar, clanged the pot onto the element, slammed the fridge door shut after finding the milk.

He'd never be able to walk away from her again. At least, not until he'd tried everything possible to win her back. That kiss, short though it had been, had proved how much he still loved her.

As if he hadn't known.

Turning the gas on to low, he stood watching the milk heat ever so slowly, thinking about Sasha and what she'd done in the intervening years when they'd both been carving out careers and turning into grounded adults. Funny how they'd both always wanted medical careers. He'd once tried to talk Sash into studying to become a doctor. She'd told him he was crazy to even think about it.

It wasn't as though she didn't have the smarts. She had as much, if not more, intelligence as any doctor he knew. Her school grades had been embarrassingly high. She'd been school dux, topped science and biology, and yet she'd refused to consider med school.

'Too big a tie,' she'd say with a grin. 'At least six years with no free time for flying, skiing or just doing.'

'Just doing' had been her favourite expression and it encompassed all things physical or fun or non-studious.

He'd argued back, 'Six years isn't all that long. And we'd be studying together.' Talk about selfish, but he hadn't been able to imagine not being all but glued to her side. If only he'd known then what the future held just around the corner he'd have kept his big gob shut.

'Two points you're missing.' She'd wagged her forefinger at him. 'It takes a lot of money to go to med school and I'm not asking Dad to fork out for me. Then there's the fact I hate being tied down too long. Can you imagine me studying twenty-four seven for years on end? I don't think so. I want to be a nurse, do the hands-on caring stuff, help people when they're feeling at their most vulnerable. I know there's a lot of study involved but not as much as it takes to become a doctor.'

He hadn't been able to argue with that and in the end he'd been the one to walk away from all their plans anyway.

The milk bubbled to the top of the pot and he deftly poured it into the large mug and stirred rapidly, swirling the dissolving chocolate through the liquid. Thinking about Sash, Sash, Sash.

Back in her bedroom the bedside light had replaced the main light, giving off a soft glow. Sash lay tucked up under her quilt, her eyes closed and her golden hair spread over the pillow. His heart felt like that chocolate in the hot milk. All gooey and swirling.

'Sash?' he called softly, in case she'd already fallen asleep.

Her eyes opened slowly. 'Hey, Grady. That smells yummy. You're spoiling me.'

Placing the mug on the bedside table, he headed for the door, where he turned to look at her. 'Get a good night's sleep, Sasha. I'll be out in the lounge if you need anything.' He wasn't leaving her in the house alone. Not after today. She'd had a huge fright and if she woke during the night he wanted to be there to reassure her that everything was fine with her baby.

Shrugging, he continued down the short hall. Who did he think he was fooling? He was staying because he had an excuse to, because he didn't want to leave her. Not until he absolutely had to—which no doubt would be tomorrow when she was back to being her normal self and kicked him out.

CHAPTER EIGHT

SASHA DRAGGED HER eyes open and peered through the gloom of her bedroom to the sunlight trying to filter in around the edges of her blinds. 'At least it's going to be a nice day, by the look of that.'

Her hands went to her stomach. 'Hey, Flipper, how're you doing in there this morning? All over yesterday's quiet spell?'

She'd fought sleep last night—and lost—afraid that she'd not notice if the baby stopped moving again. Twice she'd woken during the night when she'd tried to roll over onto her stomach and immediately she'd felt a kick from inside. The relief had been enormous, but nothing like that moment when the hospital technician had shown her the printout with her baby's heartbeat looking absolutely normal.

Didn't mean she'd stop worrying for the rest of her pregnancy, though.

Stretching her toes to the end of the bed and her arms above her head, she revelled in the sheer indulgence of lying in bed. If only it was the weekend and she could stay all snug and warm in here for another hour or so.

'Got to get up, lazybones. You've got a full load of patients today. You're not supposed to be late, remember?' And judging by the light filtering in, she was well on the way to being just that. It was as if something was testing her, making her earn this job by throwing obstacles all over the place to check her determination to turn up at work on time every day.

Reaching for her robe lying at the end of the bed, she shoved into it and headed for the kitchen. Stopped in the doorway. 'Grady? What are you doing here?'

Grady finished filling the kettle and plugged it in. 'I slept over. In case you had any more problems with baby.'

Warmth stole through her, heating her cheeks, her everywhere bits, and especially her heart.

He'd looked out for her. He'd been doing that from the moment she'd rushed into the nurses' room beside herself with fear for Flipper. She so wasn't used to this.

'Where did you sleep?' The cottage didn't run to a spare bed. She'd already started preparing the tiny second bedroom for the baby, collecting cute little knick knacks in pink, buying a bassinet and change table. Until Flipper she hadn't even liked pink. Too girly.

'Your couch folds out into a bed of sorts.' He rolled his neck and she heard it click. 'Not the most comfortable, I admit, but I managed to get some sleep.'

Now she felt indebted to him. 'You should've gone home. I was fine.' To think she hadn't known he was here. Her radar had failed. She stared at him, and the man she used to love watched her back. If that kiss was anything to go by, she ran the chance of falling for him all over again. That would be an unfortunate error on her part, because they weren't going anywhere with this fledgling friendship.

Entrusting her heart to Grady again would have

to be right up there with leaping out of her plane without a parachute. Not because he was a bad person. Far from it. His heart was in the right place. Hers had difficulty making good decisions. She seemed to have a flaw that made men leave around the time when she started to relax with them.

Admittedly, it had been slightly different with this particular man watching her from under those thick black eyebrows. She'd been relaxed and involved and in love with him from the first time they'd met. It had been a very intense relationship and she'd believed he was equally as happy until he'd walked. But he had walked, leaving her shattered and shocked.

She was beginning to understand what it had cost him to help his family, though. He'd not only forced her away, he'd put his whole life on hold, including the career he'd worked so hard for with the high grades to get him into medical school. If only she'd stopped to think it through at the time, they might've come up with some arrangement to keep their relationship working. The only good thing to come out of Mum's MS was that she'd started seeing what Grady had had to deal with. It might be too late for her and Grady, but at least she'd be more careful in the future.

With a heavy heart, she told him, 'Thanks for staying over even when it wasn't necessary. I'm going to have a shower and head into work. I guess I'll see you around over the next few days.'

His lips whitened and he shoved his hands deep into those muscle-hugging, butt-defining jeans he wore with such nonchalance. 'How about I see you in forty-five minutes' time when I pick you up and drive you to work? Your car's still at the medical centre, remember?' Then he headed away.

She stared at her front door as it closed behind that straight back and tight shoulders. 'Now I've gone and upset him.'

But it was probably for the best. She had to put the barriers back in place to keep him at a distance.

Sasha tried to relax for the fifteen-minute ride into work. Not easy with Grady less than a stretch away. He was completely focused on driving and avoiding school kids on bikes who veered out into the middle of the road. Totally ignoring her.

Finally they pulled up at the centre. She had to say something or she'd spend the rest of the day feeling terrible. 'Grady, I'm sorry. You went out of your way to help me and then I pushed you aside.' She gripped her bag. 'I made a mistake last night when I kissed you.' Though it hadn't felt like a mistake at the time. 'We need to keep our distance. You're here for such a short time and I have a lot on my plate at the moment.'

'It's all right, Sash. I get it. There's to be no rerun of the past.' Did he have to look so disappointed? Nah, couldn't be. Had to be that he was angry with her for kissing him in the first place and then making it sound like he was the problem here.

She headed inside, turning when she realised Grady was following her. 'You don't have to escort me right into my room.'

'I'm working this morning.'

Keeping that distance just got harder. 'Are you coming to the staff meeting?'

'Yep.'

Wonderful. A glance at her watch showed she had time to top up her medical kit beforehand. 'White and one, thanks.' She cracked Grady a smile. 'I'll be five minutes.'

'Yes, ma'am.'

Jess jumped up from the desk the moment Sasha walked into their room. Engulfing her in a huge hug, she sniffed. 'Told you Flipper would be all right.'

Sniff back. 'Guess that was the first of millions of crises my girl's going to cause. I hope I'm cut out for this.'

Stepping back, Jess grinned. 'Welcome to my world. Nicholas brings me so much happiness and worry all wrapped up together, it can be scary, but I keep reminding myself there are millions of kids out there with parents who feel the same and they grow up fine.'

'That's supposed to make me feel better?' She grinned back. 'I'm going to buy you a cellphone that is only to be used to talk to me, because you're my first line of defence when I can't cope.'

'I signed up for friendship so bring it on.'

Jess's grin wavered. 'You do have your parents on standby.'

Unlike Jessica. Another hug was called for. 'You know, if you called her Mum would be on your doorstep before you'd finished saying you needed help. She adores you and Nicholas.'

'Great, now look what you've done.' Jess rummaged around for the tissues. 'Sasha, you're in for the most amazing experience. Having a baby is wonderful beyond description. Yeah, it can be frightening, doing it on your own, but the rewards more than make up for that. Anyway, apparently I'll be on the end of the phone all the time. That's if I'm not glued to your hip.'

'Now, there's an idea.' She sucked in her trepidation. 'Guess we'd better get to that meeting.'

She grinned at the coffee waiting on the table. Everyone asked about her baby before they got down to the business of discussing patients.

Then Sasha told everyone about Campbell McRae and her concerns for his mental state. 'I'm going to visit him again today, more to check that he's not become any further depressed than anything else. But I did wonder if some counselling sessions might help.' Rory was Campbell's doctor.

'It would, but do you honestly see Campbell turning up for them? Especially as he'll have to drive over the hill to see anyone.'

Beside him Grady sat, tapping the tabletop with his finger. 'Want me to go with Sasha to see him? Give him a medical assessment?'

They needed to be fixing the problems she'd already noted. 'Medically Campbell's doing fine, apart from ignoring his exercise routine and letting his glucose levels creep up a little with the occasional intake of chocolate. It's the head stuff that needs dealing with.'

Rory answered before Grady even got his mouth open. 'I like the idea of Grady visiting him. The guy enjoys being made a fuss of. What bigger fuss than a doctor calling in?' He glanced at Grady, and something passed between them.

Something that made Sasha sit up. Those men were too smug. 'Grady can head up that way while I go in the other direction. He'll be saving me time when I've got a long list of patients to see today, starting up the Cobb Valley.'

What was Grady doing here anyway? It's not like he had a job at the centre. Oh, no. She shivered. He didn't, did he? He hadn't told her anything about his current job, where he worked, what he intended doing after he'd got that house ready for the market. Had she missed a vital clue somewhere between the Donovans' accident and last night's kiss?

That kiss. She swallowed a groan. What had she been thinking? And there was no way she could blame it on Flipper's little sleep that had sent her into a mad panic for hours. Her hand brushed her bump. Almost simultaneously felt a kick. *Yah, good girl. Love ya.*

Glancing around the table, she found all eyes on her. 'What?' Had she missed something? Something monumental? Like there was yoghurt on her chin?

Oh, no. It had to do with Grady. She just knew it. Worse, Grady and her. What crazy scheme were the doctors hatching? She flicked Jess a 'what's going on?' look, got a shrug in return. Traitor. Friends stuck together through everything. Break-ups, reunions, uninvited babies, family crises.

Grady cut in. 'There's a patient on your house call list that Roz wants seen by a doctor as well as you. Mary Stanners. Are you aware of her case?'

'She had a car accident last month and spent four weeks in hospital with a fractured femur and hips, a ruptured spleen and both lungs punctured. She's now at home under the care of her elderly mother.'

Roz added her bit. 'The situation worries me, Sasha. Mary should've been kept in hospital for at least another week but they were short of beds. I think it's wise to keep an eye on her. I'd also prefer it if we didn't ask her to make that long and uncomfortable drive in here until her pain level has improved.'

'Makes sense.' And keeps Grady in my vehicle. Why didn't I do midwifery instead of stopping at general nursing?

Mike added, 'We're making use of Grady while he's here. For either Roz or I to take a couple of hours to do the round trip visiting Mary takes a huge chunk out of the clinic schedule. Since

Mary is already on your list of patients, it makes sense for Grady to accompany you.'

'And this has absolutely nothing to do with my worry over lifting Josh up yesterday and hurting my back. Nothing to do with my mad dash over to Nelson last night.'

'Of course not.'

'Not at all.'

Sasha felt her brow wrinkling, and forced it smooth again. They were babysitting her because of yesterday's drama. It was kind of nice, if Grady wasn't going to be her constant companion. Her hormones were in for a long, exhausting day. But arguing with these guys wouldn't get her anywhere. She'd accept the deal for today, get on with her patient list, come up with a solution to get rid of Grady by tomorrow.

'Not a problem. We'll go and see Mary first and then I'll drop Grady back here before heading to the Cobb.' Didn't have to give in gracefully, did she?

Grady wanted to throttle Sasha and laugh out loud all at the same time. She absolutely hated to be bested, and she knew that's exactly what had happened. Mary Stanners lived less than thirty minutes from the farmlet Roz and Mike lived on. It would be no problem for one of them to call in on the way home at the end of the day. Roz had apparently been doing that every day anyway.

'I'll go get my files and kit. See you in ten.' Sasha gave him an 'I'm still in charge' glare as she rinsed her mug under the tap and placed it in the dishwasher. 'The car needs fuelling on the way out.'

'Yes, ma'am.' He resisted throwing a salute. They had to spend the day together.

'Being smug doesn't suit you,' she muttered as she pushed past him on her way out.

'Still always have to get the last word in.' His grin wavered as his nostrils filled with honeysuckle scent. Closing his eyes, he watched a rerun of the image in his mind of Sasha curled up in the front seat of his car, sound asleep. Then, bang, that kiss flashed across his brain, filled his body with heat and need. Snapping his eyes open, he strode resolutely to the office where he would find Mary Stanners's complete medical records.

Anything to keep his mind on the job and off Nurse Wilson.

'Sheree, can I please have a printout of all the hospital reports on Mary Stanners?' he asked the receptionist the moment she put the phone down after taking an appointment booking.

'Sure.' Her fingers began clicking away on the keyboard of her computer, and the phone began ringing again.

'Sheree, has the courier dropped off a package from the medical supplies company?' Sasha bounced into the office.

Damn it, woman, give me some space here. It's bad enough I'm going to be sitting in your vehicle, sucking up all that honeysuckle smell, for hours on end, not to have you following me around the medical centre as well.

Grady watched the computer screen over the receptionist's shoulder, refusing his body's command to turn and look at Sash. But he knew the instant she came to stand on the other side of Sheree. Why had he put his hand up to go on the rounds with her? What little devil had been playing havoc inside his skull this morning? He should be at home, preparing the lounge for painting, doing sensible, sane jobs that would get him out of town quickly. *If he was still leaving.* Focus on the screen, stop thinking about—anything.

Sheree glanced at Sasha and pointed a pen in the direction of a bench on the back wall of her office while talking to someone on the phone and printing off the notes he wanted. Wonder woman. Who said medical centres relied on their doctors and nurses to keep things on an even keel? Without Sheree this place would fall apart before the first tea break.

Without her he'd be negotiating his way around the alien program on the computer in the staff-room, trying to extract the notes he needed, and wouldn't be losing his mind over Sasha.

They hit the road five minutes later than Sasha had intended and headed for the petrol station. The moment she pulled up to the pump Grady hopped out and made to fill up the vehicle's tank.

'You don't have to mollycoddle me. Refuelling my vehicle is very simple. Baby brain can still manage that.'

'Go and sign for the petrol, Sasha. I'd be doing

this for you no matter what your situation.' Did he sound as tired as he felt? Probably. Sasha's eyebrows had risen at his tone.

But at least she stomped inside after a curt, 'Thanks.'

Back on the road the silence was deafening. Grady replayed the previous night and wondered where he'd gone wrong. He'd looked out for Sash all the way. Except for that kiss—which Sash had started. *Oh, yeah, of course you hadn't been thinking about kissing her, definitely didn't want to.* One step forward, ten back.

He'd concentrate on the calls they'd be making and hopefully soon Sash would relax enough to start talking freely with him. 'Who's your first patient?'

'Janice and Julie Daniels, seven-year-old twins. They've had a severe vomiting bug and their mum's keeping them in isolation. No point in spreading the bug to all their schoolmates.'

What about you? Shouldn't you be staying away from them too? Dehydration due to vomiting is not good for your baby. He bit down on the words that would cause a greater rift between them and went for, 'Has anyone else in the bay had this bug?'

The corner of her mouth lifted in a wry smile. So she'd known what he was thinking anyway. Might as well have said it.

'Not so far. Kathy Daniels thinks the girls caught it while over in Nelson with their cousins.'

'Let's hope we keep it contained.' He wasn't thinking only of the twins' schoolmates. The woman beside him was his number-one priority.

'Thanks, mate,' Sasha growled. Mud and muck splashed onto the windscreen, thrown up by the stock truck they were now following up a narrow, metal road. She flicked the wipers on and pressed the cleaning liquid button. Soapy water briefly turned the windscreen opaque and Sasha slowed, dropping back far enough not to collect any more mess. 'There's one call not on the list that we'll make after the twins. I always drop in on Mr Harris whenever I'm out this way. He's in his eighties and lives with his son and daughter-in-law. He's got a history of cardiac failure.'

'Are you talking Old Jack, the man my father used to go fishing with every Christmas Eve?'

When she nodded he continued. 'They'd get blue cod for Christmas breakfast. Dad bought the beach house from Jack when he moved up to the farm with his family. They hit it off and that fishing trip became a ritual. I'd wondered if he was still around.' The memories were warm, comfortable.

'He's as spry as a sixty-year-old. Refuses to let his heart condition dominate what he does, though I don't think he gets out fishing any more. No one to go with, and his son's always too busy with the farm.'

'I could take him out if I get a chance to put the boat in working order.'

Sasha glanced his way. 'Mr Harris would love that. So you've still got a boat?'

'The same old aluminium runabout. I tested the motor the other day. Needs a bit of TLC but nothing major.'

'At last.' Sasha slowed to a stop as the stock truck negotiated the turn onto the farm they'd been driving beside. 'Guess that's a load of beef heading for market.' She nodded towards the yards a hundred metres away by a cluster of sheds. 'Sirloin on legs. Yum.'

'Makes that chicken-and-salad-filled bread roll you bought at the service station seem lame.' And the ham sandwiches he'd bought just as unappetising.

Ten minutes later they pulled up at a large old villa sitting in the middle of immaculate lawns and gardens that spoke of many hours of weeding and pruning. 'That's stunning.'

'Isn't it? Whenever I see this I think I'd love a garden to spend time in.' Sasha laughed. 'Then I remember the only time I tried growing radishes, which anyone can supposedly grow, and how they were the biggest flop ever. I was only five but my schoolmates all grew plump, delicious radishes. Got right up my nose, that did, and I never tried again.'

'Bet they can't fly a plane.'

'True.' She slid out of the vehicle and collected her pack of supplies. 'Coming?'

Julie and Janice were very unwell little cuties who still had enough energy to sit up in their beds the moment Sasha entered their bedroom.

Grady laughed when they told him knock, knock jokes, and chuckled as they kept finishing each other's sentences, commiserated when they told Sasha how many times they'd puked.

Kids, eh? He'd not given having a family of his own much thought. Hadn't seen the point when he was seriously single. But apparently a few days around Sash made a huge difference in his outlook. Having children would be kind of cool. With the right mother, of course. Funny how his gaze tracked immediately to Sash. Like that was going to happen, no matter how patient he was and how much he tried to fool himself she might give him a second chance. Not after her warning that morning.

Sasha took temperatures and listened to their chests when Kathy said they'd started coughing during the night. 'Their temps are still a little high, but I think the worst of that bug is over.'

Grady also felt their tummies and listened to their chests. 'I'll write out prescriptions for antibiotics. I think they're both presenting with the beginning of a chest infection. Double trouble,' he said, as he handed the prescriptions over.

'Double love,' Kathy said, as she passed the prescriptions on to Sasha.

'We'll drop this in when we get back to town and then Sheree will bring it out on her way home.' Sasha clipped the piece of paper to the outside of Julie's file. 'She's Kathy's sister and lives two farms down the road.'

'Small communities have their advantages.' Grady picked up the stethoscope to place it in its pouch in Sasha's kit.

'Sometimes,' the women answered in unison, then burst into laughter.

'Not when you want to keep something secret, eh, Kathy?'

Kathy's cheeks reddened. 'You can talk, Sasha Wilson.'

'Time we were on the road.' Sasha slung the pack over one shoulder and waved at the twins. 'See you two scallywags tomorrow.'

Back in the four-wheel drive, Grady dared to ask, 'What was your great secret that the town found out about?'

'I didn't ride into town and announce to all and sundry I was pregnant. Apart from telling Mum and Dad, I kept it to myself for a while. Thought I'd give them time to get used to the idea before I started letting it out, but I hadn't counted on Kathy guessing. Not that she went wild with the news, but she made me realise I couldn't keep Flipper hidden for ever.'

'I take it they knew at the medical centre?'

'I was up front with them right from the start. Had to be. I'm there to cover Karen's maternity leave, but Mike and Rory have indicated there might be a permanent job at the end of it.' Worry darkened her words, tightened her brow.

'What will you do if the job doesn't eventuate?'

'That's not an option.' She leaned forward to peer through the windscreen, and instantly eased off on the accelerator and wound down her window. Cold air filled the cab.

'What's up?' Grady asked, as he craned his neck to see past her head.

'I'm not sure but those guys are running towards the shed, carrying someone between them.'

'I see them. That's the farm the stock truck turned into.' Unease made him wary. 'We'd better go and see if we're needed.' Men didn't usually run around with one of their mates swinging from their arms.

'On our way.' Sasha turned sharply, bounced the vehicle over the cattle stop and drove directly to the shed. 'Stock truck's still here, parked over behind that second shed.'

'Drive right up to that door where those men ducked inside.' Grady undid his seat belt, ready to follow the men.

Before Sasha had pulled up, a man appeared in the doorway, carrying a rifle under his arm. 'What the heck?' She stuck her head out the window. 'What's happening, Jason?'

'Sasha? That was quick. Murts is in a bad way. That bull went berko when we tried to load him. Got Murts in the gut I don't know how many times.' The man who was apparently Jason strode over to them. 'I'm going to put a bullet between his eyes.'

'What do you mean, that was quick?' Grady asked as he climbed out. 'We've been up the road, visiting patients, and saw you all running inside the shed.'

Jason looked across at him, then back to

Sasha, a question in his eyes. 'I phoned 111 and McKentry used his truck phone to call the medical centre. Mike's getting the ambulance and heading out here as soon as he can.'

Sasha joined Jason. 'This is Grady O'Neil. He's a doctor.'

'Some good news.' Jason pushed Grady towards the shed. 'Go, man. Murts needs you real bad.'

Grady called over his shoulder to Sasha, 'Bring your pack with you.' Not that it contained half the equipment he'd give his right arm for at this moment. He hated to think of the injuries this guy Murts had suffered every time that bull's head had slammed into his gut.

The man lying on the floor of the shed looked worse than even he'd imagined. Covered in blood from head to foot, he was shaking and groaning as his friends knelt beside him, helpless to do anything. 'Hey, guys. Grady O'Neil. I'm a doctor.'

In the shed the relief was almost palpable. As the three men scrambled out of the way they tripped over themselves. 'Thank God,' one of them muttered, then added, 'Hello, and we've got Sasha. Murts, this is your lucky day, dude.'

Unable to see anything lucky in being gored by a raging bull, Grady kept his mouth shut and knelt down on the hard dirt. Sasha joined him on the other side and immediately began taking a pulse. Make that tried to take a pulse. Her finger pressed on the carotid, moved a smidge left, right. Then, 'At last,' she whispered.

Grady spoke to the patient. 'Hello, Murts. I'm Grady, a doctor. And Sasha's here, she's a nurse.'

'Glad to see you,' the guy wheezed around his obvious pain, and opened his eyes for a brief moment.

'Murts, how old are you?'

'Forty-eight.'

A clear verbal response, and Murts had opened his eyes. 'Can you feel my hand?' Grady asked as he touched his patient's hand, and felt a small clenching around his fingers. 'GCS thirteen,' he told Sasha. Not bad in the circumstances.

'Pulse weak and low,' she responded.

Not good. Grady settled further down on his

haunches. 'Murts, can you tell me where the pain is coming from?'

'Everywhere.'

Okay. Try again. 'What about your head?'

'Yes, bad.'

'Your chest?' Grady asked. There could be a pneumothorax if that solid head had hit Murts's ribs hard enough. Or often enough.

'Agony,' Murts muttered.

Grady said in an aside to Sasha, 'How do we go about calling for the rescue helicopter?' Without that, this man was unlikely to survive. A two-hour trip over the hill was not an option.

'I imagine Mike would've put them on standby the moment he got the call. They have to come from Wellington or Nelson, about equal flying times.'

'Can you get Mike on the phone for me? Then see if any of these men saw the attack and where the bull got Murts, other than in the gut, as already mentioned.'

'Sure.' She stood, tugged her phone from her pocket and punched buttons. After handing the phone to him, she strode across to where the three men hovered anxiously.

He heard Mike answer his phone and got on with getting what he needed. 'We're with the man attacked by a bull. Can you make that helicopter a go? Needed here a.s.a.p.'

'Onto it. I'll be with you in ten.' The phone went dead.

Continuing with his examination, Grady worked his hands over the chest he'd just exposed by tearing away what remained of Murts's shirt. Beneath his hands the man writhed and groaned. Pain or cerebral irritation? What he wouldn't do for a fully equipped theatre at this moment, and an X-ray machine. Or even that ambulance with at least essential equipment.

Sash squatted down again. 'The bull rammed into Murts continually pretty much everywhere. The guys reckon at least twenty times.'

Grady closed his eyes briefly. Murts was lucky to be alive.

Sash wasn't finished. 'His head whipped all over the place, often connecting with the wooden fence rails. His legs took some hits as well.'

'So we're looking at internal injuries, possibly broken ribs and a punctured lung, and brain injuries.'

'Could be bleeding out internally, too.' Sasha began counting Murts's resp rate again.

'I need to insert an artificial airway before he gets into that helicopter. I'm presuming there are the right drugs in that ambulance so that I can do an RSI?'

'Resp rate fifty-two. Too low,' she murmured, as she looked directly at him, the worry for Murts obvious in her eyes. 'They're in the pack that Mike will bring from the surgery. As there are no ambulance personnel qualified to use most drugs, they're only carried when one of the doctors attends an incident.'

'Good policy, though right now I could do without it.'

'I think both femurs are broken,' Sasha's hands were carefully working down the length of Murts's left leg. 'We're going to have to straighten them and apply splints before loading him in the helicopter.'

'We'll wait for that drug kit and some morphine.' He began checking the right leg, working in sync with Sasha. Amazing how well they worked together. But it shouldn't be a surprise. They'd always done things well together.

A shot rang out, quickly followed by another.

Grady saw Sasha shiver and reached over to run a finger over her hand. 'Had to be done.'

'I know, but doesn't mean I have to like it.'

The men gave a cheer. 'That'll show him,' one of them muttered, as they headed outside.

'What was that you said about sirloin on the way in?' Grady asked Sasha with a smile, trying to lift her spirits.

Her face paled. 'No, thanks. Think I'll stick to my chicken now.'

'You squeamish about where your meat comes from?' He held back a chuckle. Probably get slapped hard for that.

'Not normally, but being pregnant has changed a lot of things. Like craving for prunes. Used to hate them as a kid and they were Mum's favourite fix for everything that ailed us.' Colour started returning to her face and she began counting Murts's resp rate again.

Murts gave a deeper groan than any before.

'Murts? What's going on?' Grady gently palpated the abdomen area where the man's fist was tapping. 'Pain here?'

'Ye-es. Ahh.'

The sound lifted the hairs on the back of Grady's neck. 'The ambulance is nearly here, and the helicopter is on its way. You hang in there, right? We'll get you sorted and into hospital where they can fix you up in no time.' Don't you dare die on us. Don't you damn well dare.

Sasha rubbed the back of one of Murts's hands. 'Who do you want to go to hospital with you? Sally or one of those lugs outside?'

'Sally's in Nelson, doing the shopping,' Murts wheezed.

'So one of those lugs it is. I'll go see who's available.' Sasha stood, leaned closer to Grady. 'Resp rate dropping. Now forty.' Then she headed out to find the men.

The sound of tyres on the gravel outside was very welcome, as was the bag of medical goodies Mike carried in moments later. 'Hey, there, Murts, hear that bull of yours went a little crazy.'

Sasha returned carrying leg splints and a stretcher from the ambulance, accompanied by Rebecca.

Grady shook his head at Sasha. 'What was wrong with getting Rebecca to carry that stretcher?'

Her face squeezed into a scowl. 'It weighs next to nothing.' But she did quickly place it on the ground near their patient, before handing the splints to Grady. 'I'll head off on my round now. With Mike and Rebecca here, you won't need me any more.' There was a hint of mischief in her eyes as she nailed him with a stare.

Sash thought she'd found a way to get rid of him for the rest of the day, did she? That sucked. Hurt, too, if he was honest. She really didn't want him accompanying her for the day. Did she dislike him now? No. Her kiss negated that theory. So his presence was stirring up memories or emotions she'd prefer weren't stirred up. Was that it? Hope flared, nudged the hurt aside. He could still rattle her cage. Cool. 'Guess what?'

When her carefully styled eyebrows lifted in a 'this had better be good' way he answered his own question. 'I'm coming with you to see Campbell McRae. Or had you forgotten that?'

The eyebrows dropped. But her mouth slid upwards into a reluctant smile. 'I'd hoped you had.'

CHAPTER NINE

SASHA SAID GOODBYE to Mrs Callahan and headed outside to the car. Mrs Callahan hadn't wanted Grady there while Sasha examined her hysterectomy wound.

'Call me old-fashioned but my woman's bits aren't for everyone to see.'

Sasha had smiled her understanding and refrained from pointing out that no 'woman's bits' would be on show anyway. Sixty-year-old Mrs Callahan was entitled to her privacy, though that was likely to go out the window when she started radiation for her cervical cancer next week in Christchurch. Sasha carefully picked her way over the rough cobblestones on the pathway. Such a nice, kind lady, known for her good deeds in the community, and she'd been dealt a bad card. Cancer didn't care who it attacked.

Rounding the corner of the house, she stopped.

Grady was leaning against her vehicle, talking on his phone, and looking so sexy in his thick jacket and his butt-hugging trousers.

Her mouth dried. No wonder she'd kissed him last night in her half-awake—or was that half-asleep—state. Kissing Grady had always been a favourite pastime. And what those kisses had led to. Thank goodness he'd put the brakes on before they'd gone any further last night. Had he wanted her? In that way? Or had her kiss turned him completely off her? Or her baby bump? That had to be a dose of reality for any man. Kissing a woman who carried another guy's baby had to be the biggest turn-off imaginable.

But look at him. Not just sexy beyond belief. Solid, reliable, caring. Special. Grady. The man she'd once intended marrying, intended sharing her future with.

Her head pounded. The blood beat along her veins. Exhaustion swamped her. Being tired be-yond belief made dealing with Grady too much. Too complicated, involved, difficult. One half-assed kiss didn't mean everything had been righted in her world. Far from it.

Flipper nudged her more gently than usual. 'Yeah, I know, baby girl. It's just you and me.' She continued down the path. This had been the last call. What with rampaging bulls and Campbell taking his time to size up Grady, and then not letting him go until he'd talked and talked and talked, they were very late. 'Time to head home and put my feet up.' Now she sounded like an old lady. Thank goodness Dad was home. She didn't have any energy to spare for packing citrus today.

'Murts has just had surgery to put rods in his femurs.' Grady shoved his phone into his jacket pocket as she approached. 'The head injuries are causing concern, as are his punctured lungs.'

'But he's alive.' A sigh rushed over her lips. 'That's got to be good news.' Poor Sally would be beside herself with worry.

'You okay?' Grady's eyes clouded with concern.

'Absolutely fantastic.' I've seen a guy who'd been battered half to death by a bull, a lovely lady dealing with cancer, and I had the biggest scare of my life yesterday. 'I'm just fine.' But she walked up to the passenger side of her vehicle and opened the door, hauled herself inside and hunched back against the seat, her eyes closed.

Grady, to his credit, didn't say a word, just walked round to the other side, adjusted the driver's seat and drove them back to town.

She'd rest on the way and then she'd be up to shopping at the supermarket and deciding what to have for dinner. Flipper was probably getting sick of soup and toast, or yoghurt. Monday night's meal at Grady's had been delicious and made her think she should be trying harder to cook tasty meals. But making them just for herself was a bore. And required energy she didn't have today.

'What would you like for dinner?' Grady's skin-lifting, emotion-grazing voice penetrated her fogged mind.

'Trying to decide between two-minute noodles and canned spaghetti,' she muttered. She wasn't lying. Suddenly having to stand at the stove at all seemed beyond her.

'How about sweet and sour pork with stir-fried rice?'

She blinked. 'What planet are you on? There's no Chinese takeaway around here.'

'Did I say anything about takeaways?' He flicked her a cocky grin.

'You're cooking again?' Her hand rested on the point her baby was currently toeing.

Grady's gaze dropped to her hand then returned to the road ahead. 'Didn't you know you can get sweet and sour pork in a packet? Just add water and stir.'

'I've been missing out on gourmet delights.' She laughed, her tiredness taking a step back. Grady was making her feel good. 'Any other flavours?'

'Not tonight.' As they neared the medical centre he said, 'Are you up to driving home from here? I need to get some groceries, mainly pork and rice, and then I'll come to your place to cook dinner.'

'I can manage fifteen minutes behind the wheel. I'm going to drop into the parents' on the way. They'll want to feel Flipper do her goal-kicking practice to make them totally happy all's well in there.'

'Okay if I let myself in if you're not home when I arrive?' He pulled up outside the medical centre.

'Go for it. The key's under the lemon-tree container.'

'Where I found it last night.'

Of course he had. She shook her head at him. 'Not the cleverest place to…' she flicked her forefingers in the air '…hide it, I know, but it's there for when I forget to take my key ring with me.'

Last night. When he'd driven her back from Nelson. After he'd sat with her, held her hand figuratively while she'd freaked out big time. A girl could get used to that if she wasn't careful. Last night—when she'd kissed him. Swallow. Maybe having Grady in her house again so soon after that faux pas was a mistake. Because those memories she refused to admit to were getting harder to deny by the minute.

But pork and fried rice sounded so much tastier than those two-minute noodles sitting in her cupboard. How pathetic was that? Unfair on Grady, too. Hey, he was a big boy. In more ways than one. He'd cope. He wouldn't have offered if he didn't want to do this. One thing about Grady— he didn't do anything he didn't want to.

Shuffling over to the driver's side, she reached

to pull the door closed that Grady had left open. 'See you in a while.' She crashed the gearstick into place and jerked her foot off the accelerator, sending the four-wheel drive bunny-hopping out of the car park.

'Excellent, Sasha. Now you're a ballet dancer on wheels.' In the rear-view mirror she saw Grady standing, hands on hips, shaking his head. 'So you don't like dancers. What do you like these days, Grady O'Neil? Who are the women you've dated since I last saw you? Beautiful ones, I'll bet. Exciting and fun, or serious and safe?'

Her good mood evaporated. She hated the thought of those other women with Grady. Even though she'd had other men, and had loved one a lot. Grady had been hers. But not any more.

'Hey, Dad, how was your trip?' Sasha wrapped her arms around her father and hugged tight. One of the good things about returning home was Dad hugs. They'd been a part of her life from as far back as she could remember.

'A darned sight less drama-ridden than things back here.' He squeezed her and stepped back, his eyes dropping to her protruding tummy. 'How is my granddaughter today?'

Sasha grabbed his hand and placed it where Flipper was kicking up a storm. 'She's been making up for lost time all day.' Watching Dad's eyes mist over as he felt the movement, her throat clogged with emotion. 'Melanie's doing fine, Dad. Everything's on target.' She winced as another kick caught at her. 'Right on target. I think I've got a women's soccer rep in there.'

'Melanie?' Dad whispered as he raised his eyes to meet her gaze. 'You're naming her after your grandmother? My mother?' he emphasised.

'Yes. Melanie Wilson the second. I'm giving her a lot to live up to, I know, but I'm sure she'll manage.'

Mum handed Dad a box of tissues and shunted him aside. 'My turn.' Her arms wrapped around Sasha's neck and she planted a soppy kiss on her cheek. 'That baby gave us a huge scare yesterday. When Grady phoned I had a wee cry.'

Grady. The name dropped between them. Mum would have a thousand questions. Dad might, too. They'd both liked Grady and had been hurt when he'd dumped her.

Sasha unwound Mum's arms, noting the slight tremors, and tried hard not to show any tears. No way did Mum want any sympathy, went nuts if anyone said anything about her illness. Which left Grady to talk about, and she so did not want to go there. 'Sorry I didn't phone. I was almost incoherent with panic.' She met Dad's gaze. Saw the empathy there for her predicament. 'So much for being the cool, calm nurse.'

'Yesterday you were a mother, not a nurse,' Mum told her. 'Are you staying for dinner?'

'Not tonight, sorry. It's been a long day and I really want to get home.' That wasn't a fib.

'What are you cooking?' Dad asked, his shrewd eyes watching her every movement.

'Sweet and sour pork with fried rice.' That wasn't quite a fib either.

'Where did you find Chinese food? Has a new place opened in the week I've been away?' He turned to Mum, who shook her head, turned back. 'Sasha?'

'Grady's cooking. He insisted and I didn't have

the energy to keep saying no.' Neither was that a fib.

'Good for him.' Mum grinned.

'Are you seeing Grady again?' Dad asked, a load of caution lacing his voice.

'No, Dad, I'm not. He's been doing some hours for the medical centre so there's no avoiding him. Then, Grady being Grady, he insisted on driving me over to Nelson last night.'

'Thank goodness he did.' Mum seemed determined to make the whole Grady thing a rosy picture. Did she want a father for Flipper? Did that make her prepared to welcome Grady into the family so easily?

'Look…' Sasha drew a shaky breath. 'Grady's back here to prepare his house for sale and then he's heading off again. We are not getting back together. Not now, not ever. It would never work.'

Dad laid his hand on her shoulder. 'Trying too hard to convince us? Or to convince yourself, love?'

The trouble with her father was that he knew her too well, had always been able to read her like a book, because they were so similar in character. Reaching up on her toes, she placed a kiss on his cheek. 'I'll be over to help with the avocados after work tomorrow. I'm sure they need thinning.'

'No need. We've got it covered.' Dad went to the front door with her, held it open as she stepped out into the cold night.

She noted the clear sky and the condensation in the air in front of her mouth. 'Could be a frost tonight.'

'Tread carefully, Sasha.'

As she slid back into her vehicle she knew Dad wasn't talking about the slippery steps or path.

She waved as she drove out onto the road home. And dinner with Grady. 'I'm trying really hard, Dad, believe me. But nothing seems to be going according to plan right now.'

The delicious aroma of fried rice teased Sasha's nostrils as she let herself into her cottage. She could so easily get used to this. Squeezing into the kitchen, she told Grady, 'That smells divine.'

He turned from the bench where he was stirring soy sauce and crushed garlic together. 'Better than your box of noodles?'

I shouldn't have agreed to this. The tiny kitchen couldn't hold both of them without them rubbing against each other. Crossing to the alcove that served as her dining room, she stopped. The table was set, waiting for her. 'Oh. Right.' Now what? She turned back to the kitchen. 'Do you want a beer or something?'

Grady lifted an open bottle from the bench. 'Sorted, thanks.'

Okay. Um, guess there wasn't anything to do except wait for that food that looked so good in the deep pan he was using as a wok. 'I'll go and change out of my work clothes, then.' She shot past him, ignoring the raised eyebrows and quirky smile on his gorgeous face. Gorgeous face?

Yeah, Dad, as you can see, I'm trying really hard to keep my distance.

'Don't be long. I'm almost ready.' Grady's voice followed her down to her bedroom. So ordinary, normal. Grady in the kitchen, preparing dinner, while she'd been visiting her parents. Now they'd sit down together and eat, talk about their day. Like a couple. A couple with their first baby on the way.

Yeah, Dad, I'm trying really hard.

Grady would be a super father. The kind any kid would want to rush home to at the end of school and tell him about all the things she'd done during the day. Did her baby need a father? Right from the day she popped out?

Flipper had needed one yesterday. As she'd needed Grady. Hard to imagine how she'd have coped without him being there for her.

'I'd have done what I always do—sucked it up and got on with it. Having Grady hanging around made it easier to give in to the fear and panic gripping me.'

She sank onto the edge of her bed, stared around the room she'd made cosy with the quilts she'd inherited from her grandmother. They were works of art, full of vibrant colours and intriguing patterns. Apart from the terracotta and cream-coloured log-cabin quilt on her bed there were three others in greens, blues and more terracotta lying on the chair in the corner and over the wooden clothes rack in the opposite corner. All made by her grandmother.

Closing her eyes, she could picture Grandma hand-piecing together intricate shapes of fabric, slowly, painstakingly, creating another magical quilt. Grandma. Sasha's hands went to her tummy. Melanie.

What are you going to be like, baby girl? Sweet and kind, like your great-grandma? Tough and determined, like your grandma? Daredevil and wild, like your mum and grandfather?

Please, not like Dad and me. I don't think I could bear to have to sit at home, waiting for you to return from some dangerous escapade.

This whole motherhood thing was huge. Terrifying. Exciting. Massive. Was she up to it? Too late. It had been too late since she'd gone to Fiji for a week with greaseball Freddy. Her hands gripped the quilt on either side of her butt. He might've turned out to be a waste of space but he had given her Flipper, and no matter what the future brought she'd be grateful for that. She might have to work hard at being the best mother but nothing would get in the way of her trying.

'Sasha?' Grady stood in the doorway. 'You okay?'

Forcing her hands to relax, she plastered the facsimile of a smile on her mouth and stood up. 'Perfectly fine.' Now, that was a fib.

'Dinner's ready.' He didn't move away, remained with his thoughtful gaze cruising over her. What was he thinking? Did she measure up to his expectations after all this time? Did he even have any expectations? And what did it matter? They had no future together.

'I'll be there in a minute.' Go away. Take those all-seeing eyes with you. Give me some space. You're crowding me, turning any rational thinking into a mire of questions and memories. Enticing crazy ideas to blossom in my skull. Ideas about you and me and my baby.

Picking up her trackpants, she waved them at Grady. 'One minute.'

The moment he turned away she untied her belt and let her trousers drop to her ankles. Stepping out of them, she tugged her trackies on and changed her blouse for a loose sweatshirt that downplayed her baby bulge. Trackpants weren't exactly a fashion statement, wouldn't flatter her or remind Grady of sex, but they were darned comfortable and comforting.

Did she want to remind Grady of sex? With her? Of course not. But having him thinking she looked a frump was hard to swallow, too. Those new trousers with the loose waistband looked okay if she wore a long top over them. Reaching into the wardrobe she heard Grady calling again. Too late. Frump look it was.

'That was as delicious as it smelt when I arrived home.' Sasha pushed her plate away after her second helping of rice and pork. 'I'm impressed.'

His grin was cocky. 'Wait till you taste my sea-food paella.'

'Guess I'll have to give that a miss. Seafood is out while I'm pregnant. Listeria is a concern.'

'So if I go out scalloping with Ian next week, you won't be able to eat any?' His grin just got bigger. 'You will hate that.'

'True. But the season will still be open when my baby arrives so I'll make up for any I've missed out on then.'

Grady gathered up their plates. 'Are you going to work right up until you have her?'

'Definitely. Unless something goes wrong, high blood pressure, that sort of thing. I don't see why not.' She needed the money.

'When is the girl you're covering for due back?'

'Karen's returning about a month after I'm due. Jess is going to cover for both of us during that time. Nicholas, her little boy, will have to go to playgroup every day, but that's no hardship. He loves it.'

Grady placed the plates in the sink and asked, 'Do you want ice cream? It's boysenberry.'

Still her favourite flavour. 'Low blow. How can I resist?'

Opening the freezer, he asked another question. 'What will you do for a job after your maternity leave is up? You said something about a permanent job but with Jess and this other nurse the centre won't need you, will they?'

'There's talk about me job sharing with Karen so we both have time off with our babies.' Half-pay would be better than none. Once she was more confident with Flipper she might have to look at moving over to Nelson and a full-time position, but at the moment she didn't intend worrying about that. She had saved and invested a lot of money during her years working in Dubai, though that was for a deposit on a house some time, not for everyday expenses. But enough of talking about her. 'Have you got a job to return to once your house is on the market?'

He leaned that mouth-watering butt against the bench and folded his arms across his chest. His eyes seemed to be searching her face, looking for who knew what. His answer, when it finally came, rocked her. 'There's a contract waiting for me to sign at the practice I qualified from in Auckland. But I like the idea of being a locum for a while. Being here and working a couple of shifts has got me thinking.'

'About working here?' she squeaked. 'As in Golden Bay?' Please, no. Not that. For a start, there weren't any vacancies at the medical centre. Though the three doctors were often bemoaning the fact they never got much time off.

'Would that be so bad?' He was serious.

For her peace of mind, yes, it would. She was

still getting used to being back home herself, starting to really relax and let go the past that involved city living, a big job and lots of people always in her face. People who hurt her, broke her trust.

But at the same time Golden Bay and Grady went hand in hand—for her anyway. She'd only known him since she was a teen but that year she'd met him on Pohara Beach had been big. She'd given him her heart in this place. She'd planned a future with him here.

Grady was waiting for her reply, still leaning against the bench, only now he looked as though he needed the cabinet's support. His eyes had darkened as they bored right inside her.

Hopefully he didn't see her confusion. Because she sure didn't understand her own feelings right now. She wasn't sure she couldn't trust him again. She also knew he made her feel safe, made her feel as though he'd do anything for her. Made her feel, full stop.

On the table her hands were shaking so she shoved them on her thighs out of his sight. 'No,

Grady, it's not a problem for me.' That was the biggest fib she could've come up with.

Her reply didn't make him look relieved. Not at all. 'But you'd prefer it if I didn't.'

Standing up, she crossed to stand directly in front of him. 'Grady, I'm still settling in myself. It's a permanent move for me.' She crossed her fingers. 'Mum's going to need more and more attention as the MS progresses, though hopefully that will be a while away. And I'd like Flipper to start her life in a place that teaches community values, where she has family and friends who'll always be there for her, no matter what.'

'The same things that are making me feel more comfortable than I've felt in years, and I didn't grow up here.' With his forefinger he lifted a strand of hair from her cheek and slipped it behind her ear. 'The things that remind me of you.'

Gulp. Move. Away. From. Grady. Now.

Her feet were lead weights, so heavy she couldn't shift. Lifting her gaze, she locked eyes with him. Saw a need in those cerulean orbs. A need for her. Gulp. This is not meant to be. *So move.*

He said, 'Want to go for a walk along the beach? There's a full moon tonight.'

Hello? Weren't we talking about you maybe moving to Golden Bay? 'Sure, I'd like that.' Huh? What happened to moving away from him, putting distance between them?

'Grab a coat, then. We'll cut through the properties at the end of the road. Hopefully the moonlight will be enough.'

'Almost daylight,' Sasha quipped, as she tripped over a large piece of driftwood at the edge of the sand.

Grady draped an arm over her shoulders and tugged her in beside him. 'You're supposed to watch where you're going.'

'Then I wouldn't see the stars above or the tide rushing up the beach, tossing shells in front of it.' Somehow her arm found its way around his waist. Walking on the beach with Grady brought back so many beautiful memories. 'We brought the CD player down to the beach and danced the night away. You ran the cable for it from your house through the flax bushes to the beach. Anyone coming down to join us tripped over the cord and let us know they were coming.' Giving us time to straighten ourselves up a bit.

'We fell asleep on the sand and woke up when the tide came in, soaking us. Didn't do the CD player any good.'

'We went skinny-dipping after everyone had gone to bed.'

'Except half my mates were already out here, doing the same thing with their girlfriends.' Grady laughed; a deep, full laugh she hadn't heard once since he'd turned up again in Golden Bay.

Warmth seeped under her jacket, stole through her heart. 'You used to laugh a lot.'

'We didn't have a care in the world, did we? Thought life was wonderful and couldn't understand how quickly and drastically it could change.' Removing his arm from her shoulders, he took her hand in his as they continued along the beach.

Sneaking a glance up at him, a smile curved her lips. His generous mouth that could kiss her blind was also smiling. This she had missed. Face it, she'd missed Grady and hadn't been able to replace him, no matter how hard she'd tried. Swinging their joined hands, she let go of the tension that had been gripping her for days and made the most of walking in the moonlight with the man who'd stolen her heart so long ago.

They turned for home and Grady stopped, placed his hands on her shoulders and gently drew her closer. Her body leant towards him, bending slightly at the waist, or where her waist used to be. Her lips parted as her tongue slid out over the bottom one. Like she wanted to taste him.

She couldn't resist him. It was beyond her. When his head lowered and his mouth covered hers she leaned closer. Inhaled that spicy man scent that was Grady. The scent that had been driving her nuts in her vehicle. The man who'd been waking her up, day by day, bringing her out of hibernation to feel again. To remind her of great sex, of love, of needs that had been shut down far too long. Her mouth opened under his, welcomed his probing tongue.

This is Sash. My love. Grady shifted slightly, wrapped his arms around Sash's waist and pulled her as close to his body as possible. His muscles remembered her. Especially those south of his belt. As he lost himself in kissing her, tasting her, feeling her plastered against his chest, belly, thighs, he went into sensory overload.

Forgot everything except Sash. The sweet honeysuckle scent on her skin. Her mouth that teased and tormented as it went from sweet and demure to saucy and sexy in a flash. As though he'd woken her up. Those breasts pressed against his chest were bigger than he remembered, ripe from her pregnancy. His hands itched to touch, cup them; his thumbs needed to rub her nipples until they peaked.

Her hands were holding his head so that he couldn't lift his mouth from hers. Her fingers were threaded through his hair, pummelling his scalp with their tips.

He felt something against his lower gut. What the—? Comprehension rushed in, had him peeling his lips off hers. 'Is that the baby? Did I just feel her kick?'

'You felt Flipper?' Astonishment crossed her face, dashed away the slumberous look that had been growing with the deepening of their kiss. 'Truly?'

'There was a small thud.' He stared in wonder at the baby bulge resting against him. 'Unbelievable.' He'd once had the opportunity to feel a baby's movements when he'd been doing his training, but this—this couldn't be more different. This was Sasha and her baby.

That green-eyed monster stirred. Grady pushed it right back where it had come from. He didn't own Sasha. She owed him nothing. He'd sent her packing, freed her from loving him, so he had no right to feel jealous of the man she'd obviously had more than a passing fling with. But where was the man?

Sasha pushed out of his arms, tugged her shirt up and then grabbed his hand to place it on her belly. 'Here.'

His palm on her skin, his fingers pressing against her flesh. Unbelievable. Sensory overload. Then he felt it. A nudge from inside Sash's belly. Wow. And again. 'That's… That's amazing.'

Sash was grinning like crazy. 'Isn't it? Amazing. That's going on in my tummy. My baby girl. She's something else.'

His other hand seemed to have a life of its own, reaching for Sash's face, cupping her cheek. His thumb traced over her jaw, along her chin and up to her sweet, sexy mouth. 'I have never known anything so unbelievable. This is real. Your baby. Nothing like what I learned in med school.'

She chuckled. 'I'd hope not. Though it is exactly the same really. But it is amazing. I never get tired of feeling Flipper go ballistic in there.'

'Especially after last night.'

'Exactly.' Her face contorted briefly.

'Another kick?' He slid his hand across her stomach to where her hand flattened and pressed down. 'Here?'

Her head dipped in acknowledgement. Her eyes glittered with love and excitement. 'I can't wait to meet her. To see what she looks like, what colour her hair and eyes are.' Then the glitter faded, replaced with worry. 'I shouldn't have said that. I'm tempting fate. I don't know what I'd do if it happened again.'

Wrapping his arms around her waist, he tugged

her close, enjoying that pushing stomach against his solar plexus. 'You are so lucky.'

'You think so?'

'I know so.' In more ways than one. Hell, he'd been an idiot when he'd told her to get on with her life without him.

Those lush lips spread into a wide smile. 'So do I.'

That smile hit him in the gut, sending desire spinning out of control, heating the corners of his body, his heart, where he'd been cold for eleven long years. When his mouth covered hers a groan rolled up his throat from that pool of need and spilled into her mouth. Under his lips her mouth opened further, allowing him deeper access. He tasted Sash. Her fire and sweetness, her softness and strength. And he was lost.

He had to have her. Taking her hand, he began pulling her along the beach as fast as it was safe to go in the near dark. 'We might have wonderful memories of what we got up to out here but it's winter, not summer. Let's carry this on back at your place.' As long as she didn't change her mind about kissing him before they got there.

Leaning down, he held her close for a quick kiss. Raced a few metres and stopped for another one. They ran and kissed all the way back to the warmth of her cottage.

Immediately they got through the front door he pulled her into him, as though they could melt into one. He knew only the woman in his arms. Then her breasts slid up his chest as she stretched up on her toes to push her fingers into his hair. Breasts that had swollen with pregnancy. Breasts that felt soft and yielding, yet their peaks were as hard as pebbles as they moved against his over-sensitised chest. And then they were filling his hands where he'd slipped under her bra.

Then Sash twisted in his arms, feverishly tugging her shirt over her head, reaching behind to unclip the annoying bra. At the same time her baby bump rubbed up against him and he dropped his hands to touch and feel and hold. When she stood naked from the waist up a lump blocked his breathing. 'You are so beautiful,' he finally managed to croak as his hands kept caressing her extended belly. 'Utterly beautiful.'

And then he couldn't think any more as those

small hands gripped his shirt and pulled him near. Her fingers plucked at the buttons of his shirt, working their way deftly down from his neck to his waist, exposing his chest bit by bit, her lips touching him with each new exposure.

Swinging Sash up into his arms, he strode to her bedroom and lowered her onto the bed, all the while kissing that swollen mouth, unable to break the contact.

Sash pulled her mouth free. 'Make love to me, Grady.' Her hands trembled as they unzipped his trousers and took his manhood, caressing and teasing.

He needed no invitation, had been waiting for this since the night on Takaka Hill when she'd slipped back into his life. He shucked his trousers, helped Sash remove hers, and then he was touching her intimately. She was wet for him, instantly arching into his hand.

'Sash, baby, take your hand off me.'

Her slumberous eyes blinked at him. 'No way, sunshine. I like what I'm feeling.'

'Sash,' he ground through clenched teeth. 'I won't last if you keep doing that.'

'You're not meant to. Ahh,' she gulped. 'Don't stop, whatever you do. Don't. Stop. That.' And then her body was convulsing against his hand. And still she rubbed him. And then he rose over her, pushed inside, felt her heat envelop him and knew no more except the waves of hot need exploding from him as he drove into Sash again and again.

CHAPTER TEN

SASH TUGGED THE quilt over their naked bodies
and snuggled against the hard, muscular length
filling her bed that was Grady. His arm encircled
her below her baby bump, pulling her as close to
him as possible.

Her brain was sluggish, filled with warmth and
the aftermath of their lovemaking. 'I've missed
that,' she whispered to herself. The instant inferno that always came with Grady touching
her. She'd even begun to believe it was all in her
imagination, made brighter as each year passed.
Now she knew she'd been right. And her body
wanted it again.

His hand slid over her breast to cup it. When
he stroked her nipple she luxuriated in the erotic
sensations flicking out from that point to touch
her toes, her thighs, both breasts, lips and fingers. Her tummy.

My pregnant tummy.

The reason she should not be lying naked in bed with Grady. Her baby girl would expect her not to make mistakes, did not deserve to have her mother bring a man into their lives who'd sooner or later leave them. Not even when she might be falling in love with that man again.

Oh, help. What have I done?

Sent Grady all the wrong messages for a start. Sent those same messages to her heart as well. Now she had to undo it all.

'Sash?' Grady murmured by her ear. 'You okay?'

No. No, she was not okay. She'd just made the biggest mistake of her life. Rolling out of his arms, she pushed to the other, cold side of her bed and sat up, tugging the quilt under her chin and all around her.

'Sash? What's up?' Grady sat up, too, reached to take her hand.

She moved right to the edge of the bed. 'No, Grady. Don't.'

Click. Yellow light flooded the room from her bedside light and Grady focused that steady gaze on her. 'I'm not understanding what's going on here.'

Neither did she. What had possessed her to have sex with him? Like she could've stopped. She'd been seized by such an overwhelming need for him her brain had fried and all reason had evaporated. Now she had to face reality, only it had just got complicated. 'This has got to stop. We can't do this again. It shouldn't have happened at all. We are not getting back together, ever.'

'Why not?'

Snapping her eyes shut, she prayed for control. She so wanted to hurl herself into his arms and beg him to make love to her again. But it was wrong. Completely wrong. Opening her eyes, she stared at him, forced a wave of need aside, and struggled to remain calm and focused. 'You can't possibly think we're going to have an affair while you're here?'

'Unless you're still in a relationship with your baby's father, why can't we get to know each other again? The chemistry's certainly still there.'

He wasn't listening. 'I do not want a relationship.' How blunt could she be? Did she need to bang him over the head to get him to understand? She leapt out of bed, fumbled around for her robe and shoved into it.

Grady stood, too, those thoughtful eyes watching her closely, hurt mingling with confusion as he asked, 'Are you hanging out for the baby's father to return to you? Because if you are, I would understand.'

A shudder rocked her. 'I never want to see Freddy again. Of course, if he changes his mind about being a part of Flipper's life then I won't deny him access. She deserves a father, even Freddy.' But move back in with him? No way.

His shoulders relaxed a little as he began dressing. 'Sash—'

'Stop calling me that,' she all but yelled. Being called Sash undermined her determination to stop whatever was going on between them before it got out of control. If it hadn't already. Being called Sash reminded her of so many things about Grady she did not need to remember as she fought to keep him at arm's length.

That hurt in his gaze deepened. 'Talk to me,

Sasha. Tell me what's really behind this? Do you not feel anything for me? Apart from the sex?'

Pain scudded through her heart. He didn't deserve this. Oh, he'd been doing a good job of stepping up for her lately. But she had a child to consider, to put before him or even herself. And she'd do anything for her baby. Sucking in a deep breath, she let rip. 'Just go, Grady. We are not meant for each other. Otherwise you'd never have dumped me.'

'I did it out of love for you.'

Make it worse, why don't you? 'Sorry, I'm not buying into that.' She brushed past him on the way out of her bedroom. She had to make him leave. Now. Before the threatening flood of tears won out over her precarious control. She headed straight for the front door, hauled it open, and shivered in the icy blast of night air. 'Please, go.' Her voice squeaked around that ball of tears.

He stood in front of her, his hands in his pockets, legs splayed and chest forward. His gaze was unwavering. 'I did it for you, Sasha. Believe me.'

'Really? You hurt me so much I went completely off the rails so that I nearly killed myself by pushing the boundaries too far. You did that for my own good?' She was nearly screaming at him now and the words would not stop. 'I have lived with the knowledge that the man I once loved with all my being did not love me back. Not enough anyway. He didn't want to share his pain, his family, his future with me. I was only good enough for the fun times, not the real nitty-gritty living stuff.'

His hands slapped his hips, his fingers white where they dug in, but he didn't step away from her tirade. 'I believed I was looking out for you by giving you your freedom to get on with the plans you'd made for your career and future. You own the dangerous stuff.'

'My future was with you.' Nothing had been more important than Grady.

'You'd dreamed of being a nurse since you were ten.'

'I could've trained in Nelson while you looked after your family. Did that ever occur to you? Did you ever think to ask me if we could rearrange our plans?' Her mouth snapped shut, her teeth banging hard. Her throat clogged with years of emotions. Those darned tears began falling. She had to get away from Grady. But more words spewed forth. 'Of course you didn't. Because apparently you didn't love me. You do remember telling me that, don't you? And now you have the audacity to say you did it for me.'

'I'm not denying anything. I did tell you I didn't love you because you wouldn't listen to me. I—'

'You're making it my fault now?'

'No, Sasha, I'm not.' His hands gripped tighter. 'It was a weird time. I was struggling to deal with Dad's passing, with having to put my plans on hold and step up for Mum, and then there was you. I didn't feel I could ask you to hang around waiting while I sorted my family out.'

Her heart squeezed. Not for her, but for Grady. 'You could have said what you've just said now. We might've been able to sort something out.'

'Would you have listened?'

'I'd have done anything to be with you.' Had she missed something back then? If she had, then so had Grady. He hadn't understood what her love for him meant. 'Anything.'

'I couldn't ask that of you.'

With one hand on his shoulder she pushed him out the door. 'Go home, Grady. We're done.'

That hurt was back in his beautiful eyes. 'You're sure about that?'

No. Not at all. It would be so easy to curl up against his chest and let him take over, be strong for her, love her. But the little girl kicking her tummy right now needed her to find her own strength. 'Yes, I am.'

'Meet me at the café for lunch,' Jess muttered, as she walked out of the office at the medical centre.

'Not hungry,' Sasha muttered back, as she avoided bumping into Grady.

'Maybe not, but you need some girlfriend time. You're looking like hell this morning. Twelve o'clock. Don't be late. I've got a full afternoon.' Jess disappeared down the hall to the nurses' room.

She could always rely on Jess to be honest. And bossy. 'Too honest for your own good,' she complained at her friend at midday as she slid onto a wooden chair in the café. 'What's this?' She eyed the bowls of pumpkin and bacon soup alongside the plate of freshly baked bread rolls before her.

'It's called food. Something Flipper needs.' Jess leaned back against her chair and studied her in a very disconcerting way.

'What? Have I got bird droppings in my hair?'

'What's with you and Grady this morning? It's like you're both afraid to go near each other.' No mucking about with Jess.

'Sort of.' Afraid of where another touch from Grady might lead, more like.

'Spill.' Jess spread a light dash of butter on her warm bun and bit into it. Her eyes lit up. 'Heaven. Jonesy knows a thing or two about baking bread.'

About to take the diversion and run with it, Sasha hesitated. Stirring her spoon round and round in her soup, she thought about Grady and making love and kicking him out afterwards and how she felt she'd done the wrong thing. She did need to talk. 'Grady stayed late last night.'

Jess looked funny with her jaw stopped in mid-chew. 'As in he and you did it?'

'Something like that.'

'Either you did or you didn't.'

'Yeah, we did.' Sipping the hot soup gave her time to rerun through her mind her final words to him. 'Then I kicked him out. For ever.'

'Why?'

Placing her spoon down on the plate, she gave up pretending to want to eat. 'We talked about back when we broke up.'

'That's good. Isn't it?'

Her shoulders lifted, dropped. 'Probably. But he won't accept that I'd have stayed with him if only he'd told me what was going on with his mother and sisters. He didn't want me to give up my plans for him.'

'Sounds kind of noble,' said the voice of reason opposite her.

'He didn't give me any choice, made my decisions for me.'

'I wouldn't have left him. But I guess he knew that and that's why he said he'd stopped loving me. Why didn't I think about the whole situation, Jess? Why didn't I ask him how he could say he didn't love me when a week before he'd told me he'd die if anything came between us?'

'Melodramatic, but he was only eighteen.' Jess buttered another bun. 'Same as you. I don't think we have all our brain cells functioning properly at that age, especially when hormones are involved.'

'And now I'm dealing with babymones.' Should she wait until Flipper was born to think this through? As if that would work.

'Yep. Give yourself time, spend some of it with Grady, get to know him all over.'

Did that last night. 'You mean all over *again*.' Picking up the spoon, she tasted the soup and rolled her eyes. 'This is yummy.' Maybe eating wasn't such a bad idea after all.

'Want to go to the pub one night soon? Have some fun? I hear they're doing a great milk and vanilla cocktail for pregnant women.'

A girls' night out sounded perfect right now. 'What about Nicholas? You could leave him with Mum and Dad.'

'I'll call them tonight. So we're on? Cool. Now eat some bread with that soup. It's good for you both.'

Grady hauled the rope in, hand over hand, straining as the weight of the dredge tried to defy him. 'Reckon we've got a full load in this sucker.'

Ian leaned over the side and peered down into the murky water. 'I see it. Look at all those lovely scallops. My mouth's watering already. Sasha's going to hate us for getting these.'

Sasha hates me already. A few scallops won't make the slightest difference. 'The blue cod will make up for not being allowed shellfish.'

'You think?' Ian's eyes twinkled as he took one side of the dredge and helped haul it into the boat. 'These are her favourite shellfish.'

Yeah, he remembered. She used to eat them raw while they were opening the shells, and then be back for a large helping when they'd been cooked on the barbecue.

Together he and Ian tipped their catch onto the deck, along with the seaweed and starfish also caught in the dredge. 'We must have at least a hundred good scallops in that lot.'

Jack slowly lowered to his knees and began tossing the obviously too small scallops back overboard. 'This is a good haul for so early in the season. Don't tell anyone about it.'

'This is Golden Bay. People will know before we hit the beach.' Ian hunkered down too.

'Want to do another run?' Grady looked up at the sky. 'I take that back. The weather's starting to close in. Better head for home.'

He began coiling the rope attached to the dredge, making meticulous loops in the bin before placing the dredge on top. Then he washed down the deck with buckets of salt water, getting rid of the worst of the mud and mess. A good hose down back home would finish the job. It'd also help keep him occupied and his mind off Sasha. As if that was at all possible.

'How's the redecorating coming along?' Ian asked, as he tossed a handful of large shellfish into the bucket.

'I'm over watching the paint dry, that's for sure. Painting in the cold winter air was asking for delays. I've got the plumber doing a refit of the bathroom next week.' He'd never intended doing that but on Saturday he'd walked in for a shower and found a crack in the old glass panel. Then he'd taken a really good look at the room and gone to phone the plumber. 'So much for just a lick of paint.'

Jack paused his sorting to ask, 'You doing the place up for yourself, or putting it on the market?'

'Probably selling it, if I can. I haven't used it since Dad died. It's gone backwards over the years. Needs someone living there most of the time to breathe life back into it.' But a big part of him did not want to let the place go now that he'd had time back here.

Staring out over the sea as he directed the nose of the boat for the shore, he could hear the laughter of nights spent on the front lawn of the house with his family and friends. Eating barbecued fish and scallops, drinking beer, having plain old, carefree fun. His heart yearned for that again. Yearned to be able to get up in the morning, every morning, and pull back the curtains to reveal the bay spread as far as the eye could see. To know the sea and sand would be waiting when he got home from work. To have a family to enjoy it with. To share the barbecued food again.

To have the impossible dream.

It all came back to Sasha.

CHAPTER ELEVEN

'ANOTHER WEEK NEARLY OVER.' On Friday Sasha stopped in at home for a late lunch before heading out on the rest of her house calls. Thank goodness the weekend was nearly here. Unfortunately the week had been quiet, keeping her hanging around the medical centre more than usual, stocking shelves with bandages and syringes, cleaning out her kit, doing inventories. Ignoring Grady when he turned up to do a half-day for Rory on Wednesday and again on Thursday.

'At least we had antenatal clinic this morning, eh, Flipper? Kind of fun being with other pregnant mums and doing their check-ups.' Jess had gone with Nicholas and his playgroup to visit Natureland in Nelson. 'Nicholas was so excited about seeing the monkeys he nearly wet himself. His little face was wide with excitement. Think you'll like monkeys, my girl?'

No answer from in there.

'Okay. What do you want for lunch? One of those fruit buns I bought yesterday or reheated tomato soup?' None of it sounded very appealing. 'I promise to go to the supermarket on the way home and get us some proper food.'

Her cell rang as Flipper nudged her. A glance at the screen and, 'Hi, Mike. What have you got for me?'

'Tamara Tucker, eighteen years old, has severe back and abdomen pains. She's out at Totaranui Camping Ground and doesn't have any way of getting into town to see us. I want you to head out there.'

'Totaranui?' About an hour away over a rough, narrow winding road that could be slippery at this time of year. 'She had to have got out there somehow. It's not on a main road to anywhere.'

'Tell me something I don't know. Apparently she and her boyfriend were dropped off on the other side by the charter boat and walked across to the camping ground where friends were supposed to have joined them for a few days.'

'The friends haven't turned up.'

'You've got it. Now, Sasha...' Mike's tone changed, turned quiet and calm.

What was she in for now? Bumps lifted on her skin. 'Ye-es?'

'Can you pick up Grady on your way? He's getting ready as we speak. Just in case this is an emergency.'

She'd seen it coming the moment Mike's tone had altered but that didn't prevent the punch to her gut. Grady. In the car with her. For an hour. And another hour on the way back. *Suck it up, girl. This is your job.* 'On my way. Will keep you posted once we get to Totaranui in case we need outside help. Is the warden there?'

'According to Tamara's boyfriend, he left early this morning for supplies in town. There aren't any other campers either.'

'Who in their right mind would be out there at this time of year?' Sasha asked Flipper, as she stuffed two buns in a plastic bag and filled her water bottle. 'At least I don't have to decide what we're having for lunch.'

Outside Grady's house she tapped the horn but he didn't appear. Climbing out of the Jeep, she stomped up to the wide-open front door. The smell of fresh paint hit her. No wonder all the windows were also open. The house would be freezing inside but getting the paint dry was obviously a problem. 'Grady? You ready?'

Silence.

She'd taken one step inside when Grady appeared, striding out of one room on the way to the kitchen. Rubbing his hair with a towel. Naked as the day he was born.

She stared, unable to even blink. Her mouth dried as she took in the sight of moving muscles, that wide chest with its sprinkling of fine black hair, of a washboard stomach, of his male tackle. Two weeks ago she'd slept with him, had had him inside her, and yet nothing measured up to the sight filling her eyes. He was stunning. He'd filled out into a very beautiful man from the teen he'd been last time she'd known him.

'Grady,' she squeaked, as he reached the kitchen doorway.

Unfortunately he heard her, because she hadn't intended making her presence known.

Grady stopped, leaned back to look directly

at her. 'Sash. I didn't realise you'd be here this soon.'

Obviously. 'I'll wait for you outside.' She ran to her vehicle, leapt in and slammed the door. His image followed her, filling her head, sending her hormones into a riot of activity, heating the chill that had lain over her since she'd sent him away. Ten minutes ago she'd thought having to ride with Grady would be difficult. Now she knew it would be impossible.

What was she supposed to do? A young woman needed help from both of them. Somehow she'd have to dig deep and pull on a mantle to hide behind for as long as this job took. She couldn't do it. She had to. It was impossible. Tough. Do it. Now. Before Grady comes out of that house and gets in beside me.

The passenger door opened and Grady's large frame, fully clothed, filled the periphery of her view. 'I'd been sanding the table and was covered in dust when Mike rang. Thought I'd have time for a shower before you turned up.'

As far as an explanation went she couldn't fault it. Didn't make the trip into Totaranui any easier, though. Funny how, even when concentrating hard on the difficult road, she still had that image of Grady firmly in the front of her head.

They hadn't even come to a stop when a young man ran towards them from a nearby hut. 'Am I glad to see you. Tamara's in a lot of pain. Screaming and crying all the time.'

Grady hopped out and extended his hand to the young guy. 'Grady O'Neil, doctor, and this is Nurse Sasha Wilson. You are…?'

The lad's hand shook when he gripped Grady's hand. 'Sorry. Tamara's boyfriend. Kevin Sparkes. She thinks it's her appendix. She's got a rumbling one or something.'

'Right, Kevin, how long has Tamara been having pain? And where is it centred mostly?' Grady took the medical kit off Sasha and ignored the scowl she gave him.

Kevin began filling them in with details as he led them to the cabin he and Tamara had hired. 'Man, she's hurting, curling up with the pain at times. I was real frightened, man. Especially when she started getting worse. Didn't know what to do. There's no one here.' He waved a hand around the camp site. 'No one.'

'You did the right thing phoning the medical centre.' Sasha trotted along on Kevin's other side.

In the cabin Tamara lay across the bunk; a large girl dressed in loose trackpants and sweatshirt. She was moaning and gripping her stomach. Then she stopped, breathing deeply.

Grady figured he knew what the problem was immediately but had to approach Tamara and her situation delicately. After he'd introduced Sasha and himself, he waited while Sasha went through the motions of checking her pulse and BP. The loaded glance Sasha gave him as she said, 'All normal,' told him she was onto it, too.

Sitting on the edge of the bunk Grady asked, 'Tamara, is it all right if I lift your top and feel your abdomen area?'

The girl nodded. 'What do you think is wrong with me?'

Uh-huh. His hand felt the contraction as Tamara suddenly gasped and snatched at Kevin's hand. A scream filled the small room, piercing in its intensity. Grady waited, nodding at Sasha who'd grabbed the girl's other hand.

When the contraction had passed, Sasha asked quietly, 'When did you last have a period?'

'Why?' Tamara blinked. 'I don't remember. I'm never regular. What's that got to do with anything anyway? This is my appendix, right?'

Grady drew a long, slow breath. 'You're having a baby, Tamara.'

The girl stared at him as though he'd lost his marbles. 'No way. That's not possible. I'd have known. You can't just have a baby and not know. I'm not stupid.'

Sasha still held her hand. 'No one's saying you're stupid. If you don't have regular periods then you wouldn't necessarily notice when you missed them. Have you had one in the last few months?'

'Yes, of course I have.' But Tamara's focus was directed on the wall behind them. Tears were oozing down her face. 'I must have.'

Kevin spoke up for the first time in a while. 'A baby? We're having a kid? No way, man. We're too young. I haven't even got a job. No, can't happen.' He pushed Grady out of the way and hauled his girlfriend into his arms. 'I'll get you to another doctor, Tam. This is crazy.'

Another contraction rippled through Tamara and she screamed louder than ever, holding onto Kevin as though her life depended on him.

As soon as the pain faded Grady said, 'I know you don't want to believe me but think about it. You're having contractions. That's what the pain is.'

Sasha added, 'I've been timing them and they're quite close. We need to examine you internally, Tamara. Are you okay about that?'

The girl nodded slowly, gulping as more tears splashed down her pale face. 'I guess. Um, it feels like I have to push my stomach out. Is the baby trying to come out?'

'I imagine so,' Grady told her. 'Let's take a look and then we'll know what's going on.' So much for a lead-in time while everyone got a little bit used to this unexpected situation. How hadn't Tamara detected any changes in her body over the previous several months? She was a large girl but she must've noticed some weight gain. Glancing across at Sasha, he saw her doing that tummy rub thing and looking a little baffled at the situation. Hadn't Tamara felt the baby kicking?

Hell, she won't have had any bloods taken for blood grouping or antibody checks. Too late now. He'd cross his fingers and hope for a normal delivery with no hidden problems. Because, even without looking, he doubted they had time to get back to Takaka before this baby made an appearance.

Sasha helped Tamara remove her pants and gently settled her back on the bunk before placing a glove-covered hand on her knee. 'I know this isn't easy, Tamara, but try to relax. Let your legs drop wide. There, that's it. Dr O'Neil will examine you. Are you all right with that?'

'Yes,' she whispered, and grabbed for Kevin's hand again.

One look and Grady turned to Sasha, asking, 'Have you got a sterile blanket in your medical kit?'

'We always carry one in a sealed pack, in case of exactly this. Not that I ever thought I'd have to use it.' She shook her head. 'I can't imagine...'

The look of disbelief in her eyes made him want to haul her in tight and reassure her. She'd done everything right so far. Sash didn't turn a blind eye to the tricky things life threw at her. No, she pulled those shoulders back and straightened her spine to face the world head on. 'Sasha, get the blanket, will you?' Grady nudged her towards the door. 'Quickly,' he added quietly, so as not to panic Tamara. 'I don't think we've got long to wait.'

Tamara went rigid as another contraction hit. This time she held back her scream, instead burying her face in Kevin's shirt. Almost as though now she knew what she faced the fear generated by the pain had gone. But she'd have more fears later when her situation really sank in.

Kevin seemed to be in total shock, barely managing to hold Tamara as she clung to him. 'We need to get to a hospital. She can't have her baby here.'

These two were barely more than kids themselves, and they'd just learned they were about to become parents, that life as they knew it was over for ever. Or had they even got that far yet? Probably not.

'The baby's head's crowning,' Grady told the young couple. 'That means it's coming out. We don't have time to take you back to town.'

'What? You mean Tam's having the baby here? But she can't. That's wrong. What if something goes wrong?'

'It won't,' Grady told Kevin. 'Now, this is how you can help Tamara.'

And they got down to the business of delivering a baby in a cabin in the back of beyond. It happened so fast no one had time to raise any more doubts.

Soon Grady was handing a tiny baby into Sasha's safe hands and the wrap she'd found in her bag of tricks so she could clear the airway and wipe out his mouth. 'Tamara, Kevin, congratulations, you've got a little boy.'

Kevin whistled. 'A boy. How cool's that, man?'

'A boy? Truly?' Tamara's eyes followed every movement Sasha made with her baby. 'It's Jordan. He's come back.'

'Who's Jordan?' Grady asked.

'My little brother.' Tamara stared at the baby, hunger filling her eyes. 'Let me see him. Can I hold him?' Tamara tried to push herself upright.

Grady leaned to give her a hand. 'Not too far. The afterbirth's coming.'

Kevin filled them in. 'Jordan was killed when Tamara's aunt backed over him in the driveway. No one in her family's been the same since.'

Sasha froze for a moment. 'That's utterly terrible.' Then she resumed checking the baby's vitals. He gave a little cry. 'There you go. His first cry. He's so cute. Here, Tamara, meet your son.' Tears streamed down Sasha's face as she, oh, so gently placed the baby in his mother's arms. 'He's just beautiful. Look, ten toes, ten fingers. And look at all that dark hair.' The tears became a flood before she turned and ran outside, banging the door behind her.

Tamara and Kevin didn't even notice, they were so absorbed in their baby. Grady cleaned up as best he could and then said, 'I'll give you a minute to yourselves,' and headed out to find Sasha leaning against the car, sobbing her heart out.

Grady placed an arm around her shoulders,

tugged her close, handed her a fistful of tissues he'd snatched from her medical kit on the way out. 'Hey, look at you. If you're like this for Tamara's baby, what'll you be like when Flipper arrives?' He grinned down at her. Swallowed at the awe glittering in her eyes. 'Guess seeing this is different for you now.'

'When I was training as a nurse and saw babies being born I never knew this tugging of the heart. I fell in love with each one but...' She waved a hand in the direction of the cabin, 'Oh, wow. He's so cute and tiny and vulnerable and helpless and all covered in mucky stuff.'

'Yep, all of those. And some.' Her body shook against him and he wrapped her closer, rubbed her back in circular motions to ease the tightness he felt in her muscles. 'And very special. Just like Flipper is.'

'How are those two going to manage?' she sniffed. 'They didn't even know.'

'Yes, well. It's kind of sad. But who knows? They could step up to be the best parents ever.' Grady continued to rub her back. 'I wonder where they come from? They've obviously been through a huge trauma with her brother.'

'We need to get them to Takaka and in touch with their family. This baby's arrival might be what they all need.' There was a waver in her voice, and under his hands he felt Sasha straightening, stiffening her shoulders, putting on her brave face again. The moment of tears was over.

Dropping a kiss on the top of her head, he stepped away, and instantly felt cold. Sash was such a part of him he didn't know how to stop missing her whenever he wasn't touching her. Which was almost all the time, especially since they'd made love and she'd kicked him out. Hell, he missed her all the time, full stop.

'You sure you're okay?'

'It's babymones.' He must've looked blank because she explained. 'Pregnancy hormones. A Jessica word. They knock me sideways at the most unexpected times. Have me crying and doing things I shouldn't be doing.'

Like making love with me. It hung between them. He could see the truth in her eyes before she turned for the cabin. She was blaming her hormones for giving in to the need that had rolled through her the other night. Newsflash, Sash. Sex was all about hormones, too. And love, and being with someone special. He must have babymones, too. Because he sure hadn't been in control that night either.

Sasha yawned and stretched. Where was she? Peeling her eyes open, she stared at the interior of her car, then looked outside at the house she was parked in front of. 'That's Colleen Simmonds's house, Flipper. How did I get here? Did you drive?'

Right then the answer appeared at the house's front door. Everything clicked into place. 'Grady.' He'd offered to drive her on her rounds after they'd dropped Tamara, Kevin and the baby at the maternity unit in town.

'Sleeping Beauty awakes.' The vehicle rocked as Grady slid behind the steering-wheel. 'Well timed. We're finished for the day.'

'I'm sorry. Don't know what came over me.' Sasha yawned. Had she really slept through the whole round? Couldn't have. But she'd been exhausted. This was going to look bad when Mike and Rory found out. Not the way to impress them. It would be another black mark against her when her performance assessment came up. That permanent job seemed to be slipping ever further away. 'Why didn't you wake me?'

'You needed the sleep and I can handle a few dressings and BP readings.' He gave her that gut-crunching grin. 'Just.'

'Thanks. But there's a problem. The doctors at the centre are hardly going to give me a permanent job if I don't do the one I've already got properly.'

'They don't need to know any different.'

'Right, Grady. This is Golden Bay, not Auckland.'

'True.' He seemed damned pleased with himself as he drove.

'Okay, I admit I'm grateful. Thank you.' She'd deal with Mike and Rory on Monday.

Then Grady pulled into his drive, and turned to look at her. 'Would you like some blue cod for your dinner? Freshly caught this morning.'

She should say no. It wasn't fair to banish

Grady from her life and then take the fish out of his hands. But who turned down fresh blue cod? She licked her lips. 'Yes, please.'

Grady's eyes seemed stuck on her mouth. When was she going to learn not to do things like that around the man? His eyes were lightening with desire that in turn sent shivers of desire over her skin. Take control, Sasha. Get the heck out of here.

No way was she sliding across from one side to the other while he sat gawping at her. Shoving her door open, she stepped out to go round the front of the car. But her action had distracted that gaze. Grady was out of the car and striding up to his front door. 'Come inside while I put the fish in a bag.'

She shouldn't go in there. The house wasn't big enough for the two of them. Seemed her feet had other ideas because she quickly found herself standing in the lounge, looking around at the new paintwork. A soft terracotta shade covered the walls, making the room feel warm despite all the windows being open. It was lovely, inviting.

'What happened to the Spanish White colour?' she called through the door.

'It was too neutral for my taste.' Grady stood in the doorway, watching her. 'Don't you like it?'

'I love it.' But what colour he painted his house had nothing to do with her. She picked up a glossy brochure. Kitchens. Flicking through the pictures and plans, it seemed awfully exciting to be revamping a house.

'I like the first and third designs. What about you?' Grady stood in front of her.

Flicking back and forth, she decided, 'Definitely the second one. More workable bench space and all the cupboards seem to flow into one another better.'

His lips pressed together as he nodded. 'I'll take that on board. Now, come and look what I've done with the dining table.'

She followed him outside to the shed where the large table that held so many memories stood. 'You've sanded it back to the wood.' She ran her hand over the smooth surface. 'That's going to come up beautifully.'

'Isn't it? I'm pleased with the result so far.' There was a ton of pride in his voice.

Why would he go to all that trouble if he was going to sell it with the house? Why had he changed his mind about paint colours when he'd said he wanted to attract as many potential buyers as possible? Why look at new kitchens? Her stomach sucked in on itself as the truth hit her hard. 'You're staying.' She shook her head from side to side. 'You're going to live almost next door to me.' *Just when I'm settling down and coming to grips with my new lifestyle.*

She'd never be able to get him out of her system this time if she had to see him every day. 'Have you taken a job at the medical centre? Is that what this is all about?'

'Thanks a lot, Sasha,' Grady drawled. 'You really know how to make a guy feel good.'

'Why now, Grady? Why can't you let me have this one little piece of New Zealand? I'm trying so hard to make this work for my baby and me. All I want is to be safe, secure and able to bring my baby girl up in a good community. But you're not going to play fair, are you?' Gulp. 'Do you think I'll let you back into my life? Just go away, Grady. Leave me be.'

Uh, hadn't she been the one to kiss him? Heat swamped her cheeks. She probably had been out of line but this was too much. 'I'm going home.'

Before she'd made it to the car Grady called after her. 'Sash, I'm not staying permanently. I'll be heading back to Auckland on Sunday. For now this is going to be my holiday retreat.'

Don't call me Sash.

Grady sank down on his haunches and watched Sash leave, speeding away to put as much distance between them as possible. His heart banged painfully in his ribcage. His head pounded behind his eyes.

'I love you, Sash. More than ever.'

She'd socked it to him about not wanting him in her life. He hadn't been expecting miracles but those words had stabbed him, sliced his heart open, exposed his needs, showed how pointless this all was.

So much for coming here and getting his life sorted so he could move on. Finally he understood totally that he didn't want to sell his house and all the memories that went with it. For the first time in eleven years he was comfortable with his father's death, could enjoy recalling all the fun times. So he'd keep the house and visit once or twice a year. If that gave Sash peace of mind then that's what he had to do.

There'd been so much hurt and confusion in those brilliant emerald eyes as she'd yelled at him, her hands on her hips, her breasts pushed forward.

He'd seen that hurt once before. The day he'd told her he didn't love her. She'd loved him then. Did that hurt mean she loved him now? How was he to know? There hadn't been any real indication.

Oh, yeah?

She'd instigated more than one of those scorching kisses.

She'd been more than happy to take him into her bed.

She'd let him feel Flipper kicking.

She'd been more than grateful he'd gone with her to Nelson when Flipper had stopped moving, even gone so far as to acknowledge she'd wanted him there.

Yet when it occurred to her he might be staying, she'd flipped her lid and told him in no uncertain terms to go someplace else.

Yeah, and what am I doing about it? Walking away, heading to Auckland in two days' time. For her sake. Doing the same as I did last time. What happened to standing tall and trying to make things work? Sash might love me, she might not. But I'm never going to know if I leave.

He'd never stopped loving her, had spent years trying to find her match and failing miserably every time. 'I love Sash Wilson. End of. And I'm going to fight for her. Patiently. One day at a time. One hour at a time. But first I have things back in Auckland to sort out.'

CHAPTER TWELVE

SIX WEEKS LATER Grady walked out of the Nelson Airport terminal and across to the aero club, where Ian waited with his plane. 'Thanks for this, Ian. I could've got a rental car.'

'Nonsense. I enjoy taking the old girl up for a spin. Don't do it often enough these days. Climb in. I've done the checks.'

Grady latched the door shut, buckled the seat belt and slipped the headset over his head. The last time he'd flown in something so small had been with Sasha the day of her sixteenth birthday when she had officially been allowed to take passengers. The calls Ian made to the control tower to report his start up were so familiar.

As the older man taxied the plane across the grass towards the runway, Grady asked, 'How's everything in Takaka?' How's Sash keeping? Is she taking it quietly now that she only has a few days to go before giving birth? Has she missed me?

'Sasha's fine. And behaving—for her.' Ian changed the subject. 'Those builders you employed have been working their butts off. You're going to be amazed at the changes.'

I hope I'm doing the right thing. 'I hear there was a hold-up with the new kitchen and that they're working overtime this weekend to finish it.'

'It's all hands to the fore tomorrow to lift two of those units inside. That's a big kitchen you've got there, son.'

Son. If only. 'It's the kitchen Sasha liked when she was flipping through the catalogue.'

'Yeah, I figured.' Ian stopped talking to him to call up the control tower again and Grady sat back to enjoy the flight over the hill. In the weeks he'd been in Auckland he'd missed Golden Bay and the relaxed lifestyle. He'd missed Sash even more. He'd been gutted eleven years ago when he'd sent her packing, but this time had been so, so much worse. He loved her in so many ways, for so many things. He did not want to go back to life without her. He was being patient, but patience sucked big time.

'Virginia's cooking you dinner tonight. We're looking after Nicholas while Sasha and Jess have their fortnightly girls' night. It had been arranged before we got your call to say you were coming down.'

Grady sucked in on the wave of disappointment rolling through him. He could wait another day to see Sash. Just. 'I look forward to dinner.' How lame did that sound? But what else could he say? Virginia and Ian had gone out of their way to make him feel at home with them, which on a positive day he took for a good sign.

He stared down at the sun-kissed waters of Tasman Bay as they flew along the coastline. So different from the icy night he'd first bumped into Sash again. Ian had opted for the long way round instead of going over the hill. Ahead he saw Totaranui and the camping ground, which prompted him to ask, 'How's Kevin settling in with helping Virginia on the orchard?'

Ian grimaced. 'He's got a lot to learn but I think he'll come right. His heart's in the right place. He wants to provide for his unexpected family.'

It had been a surprise for everyone when Kevin and Tamara had decided they wanted to live in Takaka with little Jordan, and not return to Christchurch to her family. 'At least he's stepping up for them.'

Which was a hell of a lot more than Sash's Freddy had done. But if he was honest he was kind of glad about that. He'd hate it if Sash decided she had to marry the guy because he was her baby's father.

Ian was still talking. 'I like that Kevin's there for Virginia. I hate that she might do something strenuous when I'm not around. Thank goodness I've only got a few months before I quit the job.'

'The Wilson women can be so stubborn.' Grady grinned across at this man who'd accepted he was trying to win over his daughter.

'Forget that at your peril.' Ian grinned back, before preparing to land at Takaka's minuscule airstrip.

Sasha walked out of Grady's house with Jess right behind her. The workmen were about to lift the huge main unit into place and had asked the women to get out of the way for their safety.

Grady apologised, looking very disappointed when Sasha told him she'd be off home. 'You just got here.'

'I'll call in again later. Jess has to pick up Nicholas from his friend's house.' Shock still held her in thrall. Had to be why she'd made that promise, but the relief in his eyes had been worth it. But 'Why did he choose that particular kitchen style?' she asked Jess when they were in the car.

'Why wouldn't he?'

'It's the one in the brochure I liked.' Sasha shook her head, trying to clear it. Grady had rung that morning to invite her over to see how his house was progressing. Like an idiot, she'd given in to temptation. She'd missed him more than she'd have believed possible. To the point she had even looked at airfares to go up to Auckland for a weekend. But Flipper was too close to arriving and she'd had to be sensible. Another first.

Jess chuckled. 'The guy will try every trick in the book to get you back.'

Sasha rubbed her lower back before getting into the car. 'You reckon?'

'Yep. He's up front about wanting you. Now all you have to do is admit that you love him, too.'

'If only it was that easy.'

Jess slapped the steering-wheel. 'Sasha, when are you going to learn? It is that easy.'

'You've been in this situation?' Sasha rubbed her back again. It ached like crazy.

Jess ignored her question. 'Grady's nothing like he was when his dad died and he had to cope with his responsibilities. His mother and sisters needed him then. I know you did too but give the guy a break. He was only eighteen and trying to do the best for all of you. Now he could cope with all of that and some.'

'I get all of that.' Really got it. To the point she didn't understand why she was stalling.

'You're made for each other.' Jess went on and on.

Sasha tuned out. Until an icky sensation of moisture made her mutter, 'Jess, shut up. My waters have broken.'

'What? They have? In my car?' Jess shook

her head and pulled to the side of the road. 'No, you're wrong. I'm the midwife. I'll tell you when your waters have broken.'

Sasha gaped at her friend gone mad and started to smile. The smile stretched into a grin, and then she was laughing hard enough to bust her sides. 'Jess, you idiot.' Laughter poured out. 'Don't stop here. Get me somewhere.'

Jess had turned in her seat to stare at her, her eyes shining as she began laughing, too. 'What's funny?'

'I don't know. I'm having a baby? Like now. In your car.'

'You can't. I— We— Okay, what should we do?'

More laughter burst out of Sasha. 'Aren't you the midwife around here?' Then pain struck and the laughter disappeared. 'Oh. My. God. That really hurts.'

Jess immediately started driving again. 'We'll go to the birthing unit and I'll time your contractions. Though it is much too soon for the baby to come. You've only just started. There's a way to go yet.'

'Watch out for those bumps. They hurt.'

Jess waved a hand at her. 'If I go any slower the car will stall.'

'Seems too soon to go to the unit.' She hadn't really started full labour, had she?

'What else are we going to do, then? We can't just creep around aimlessly. One of Toby's men will lock us up in the police cells for loitering.'

Another pain gripped Sasha. Her hands clasped her belly. 'Call Grady. Now.'

Through every contraction Grady held Sasha with his strong arms as she stood, leaning into him. It was the most comfortable position she could find. Which was excruciatingly painful. His hands rubbing her back soothed, irritated, comforted and annoyed her. He took it calmly and reasonably when she had a momentary loss of sanity and swore at him. Then when she blamed men in general for her predicament he hugged her.

He never left her side for the fourteen hours Flipper took to make her entrance into the world.

Tears were streaming down Jess's face when

she finally handed over the precious bundle. 'Say hello to your beautiful baby girl, Sasha.'

Tears poured out of Sasha's eyes as she hungrily peered into the folds of the soft pink wrap to see her daughter. 'She's so beautiful.' She repeated Jess's description. 'So, so beautiful,' she whispered as a humongous lump clogged her throat.

Tears slid down Grady's cheeks too as he leaned over to get his first glimpse of her little girl. 'Hey, gorgeous, you look just like your mum. Beautiful.' He choked out that last word and smeared the tears across his face with the back of his hand.

Sasha smiled at him and went back to studying her baby. Her baby felt so light and tiny and yet real and precious. 'Hello, Melanie. I'm Mummy.' Then she couldn't utter another word for all the love clogging her throat.

Grady's hand curved over her shoulder, squeezed gently. 'Your mummy is going to be the best in the world, Melanie. You are a very lucky girl to have her.'

She couldn't remove a hand from her baby to

touch him. Not when she'd waited so long for this moment, to hold Melanie, but she managed to look up into his eyes and smile. 'You reckon?'

'I know.' His return smile cracked her heart wide open.

So wide that she could no longer hold onto her doubts about him. Not when she didn't believe them any more, hadn't for months, if she was honest. No, now she wanted to show him how much she loved him. Words alone wouldn't cut it. There was only one thing she could give him at this moment that showed her true feelings. 'Grady, would you hold Melanie?'

His face lit up as though she'd given him the best gift possible. 'Can I?' His mouth split into a big grin as he ever so carefully took her baby from her arms and held her to his chest, his hands enormous against the small baby. His eyes were filled with wonder as they fixed on Melanie, drinking in the sight of her. And those tears started again, fatter, faster this time. 'Hello, sweetheart. Anyone told you how cute you are?' he whispered.

Sasha felt her own eyes watering up again.

What a perfect picture. Grady holding Melanie as though he'd give his life for her. Which he would. Without a doubt. Her body was exhausted and yet exhilaration sped along her veins. Now she really was a mum. For ever. There'd be no going back. 'I'm a forever mum.'

Grady raised his head, locking those love-filled eyes on her. 'Goes with those forever legs.'

More tears slid down her cheeks. She'd turned into such a crybaby lately. Running her hands down her cheeks to wipe them away, she said, 'Guess these aren't babymones making me topsy-turvy any more.'

'You reckon?' Jess grinned. 'I'm going to head out for a while, give your parents a call while you three have some family time.'

'Family?' Her lungs stalled. Family. Yeah. Her gaze tracked back to Grady, found the same stunned look in his eyes as must be in hers. 'Family,' she whispered to him as the door closed quietly behind Jess.

Wariness filtered into his gaze. 'Sash? What are you saying?'

'I love you.' Okay, that was little bit blunt. 'It's

taken me a while to admit it. I've been holding out for some crazy, inexplicable reason, denying it to myself.'

'Babymones,' he croaked.

Laying her hand over the one of his that rested on Melanie's blanket, she shook her head. 'That's an excuse. I've hung onto the fact that you dumped me for too long. If I'd been more mature, less self-centred that day, I might've seen what you were doing. I should've seen your pain and dilemma.'

His hand turned over to wrap around hers. 'Neither of us knew how to cope with everything going down at that time.'

Squeezing her fingers around his, she told him, 'Maybe, maybe not. But I know we can manage anything thrown at us now if we're together. I love you so much.'

'Patience. I knew it.' A hint of smugness?

'Pardon?' She smiled at this wonderful man.

'I had to keep putting the brakes on my need for you. I'd have had you in my bed that same night we met on the hill if I'd had half a chance. I had missed you so much it hurt. But it was like putting my hand in the fire every time I tried to get close. So I kept telling myself to be patient, take my time, and hopefully I'd win your trust, your heart.'

'You do love me.' Relief and happiness and excitement poured through her, made her hands shake.

'Never stopped. I admit to trying bloody hard to forget you, but some things are impossible. You're a part of me, Sash.'

'I love it when you call me Sash.'

'I know.'

'Looking smug doesn't suit you.' She grinned and leaned in for a kiss, careful not to squash her baby girl between them. 'You're looking quite the dad, too.'

Grady looked as though he never wanted to let Melanie out of his arms. 'She's lovely. Hello, Melanie Wilson.'

Sasha said quietly, 'Melanie O'Neil.'

Grady's eyes bored into her. Did he think she'd finally gone totally bananas? She drew air into her lungs, reached for Grady's hand, locked gazes with him and said loudly, clearly, 'Why not? I love you. So…' Her voice faltered. Huffing out the breath she'd been holding, she drew another and quickly asked, 'So will you please marry us?'

Melanie was placed, oh, so carefully in the baby crib and then Sasha gasped as Grady scooped her off the bed and into those strong, safe and trustworthy arms.

'Typical Sash. Got to get the first word in.' He grinned. 'That had been my next question for you.' His lips brushed hers. Teasing, tantalising. 'My answer is…' He stopped to kiss her, more thoroughly this time. 'Yes. I love you so much, Sash. So, yes, try stopping me now that you've asked.'

Sasha kissed him this time. 'I won't be stopping you. I think I've done too much of that already.'

Their kiss deepened, holding so much love and promise Sasha knew winter had gone for good. Finally tugging her lips away from that wonderful mouth, she asked, 'Let's have a summer wedding. Just a small one.'

Grady groaned. 'You've never done anything small in your life, Sash. Why start now?'

There was a tiny cry from the pink bundle in

the crib beside her. Sasha reached in and lifted her daughter out, feeling her breasts tighten in response. Oh, my. This motherhood thing was amazing. Her baby might've left her body but they were still so connected. 'They don't come much smaller than this.' She grinned at him through another deluge of tears.

'You done good.' He grinned back. 'Summer wedding it is.'

* * * * *

Mills & Boon® Large Print
Medical

January

200 HARLEY STREET: THE SHAMELESS MAVERICK	Louisa George
200 HARLEY STREET: THE TORTURED HERO	Amy Andrews
A HOME FOR THE HOT-SHOT DOC	Dianne Drake
A DOCTOR'S CONFESSION	Dianne Drake
THE ACCIDENTAL DADDY	Meredith Webber
PREGNANT WITH THE SOLDIER'S SON	Amy Ruttan

February

TEMPTED BY HER BOSS	Scarlet Wilson
HIS GIRL FROM NOWHERE	Tina Beckett
FALLING FOR DR DIMITRIOU	Anne Fraser
RETURN OF DR IRRESISTIBLE	Amalie Berlin
DARING TO DATE HER BOSS	Joanna Neil
A DOCTOR TO HEAL HER HEART	Annie Claydon

March

A SECRET SHARED...	Marion Lennox
FLIRTING WITH THE DOC OF HER DREAMS	Janice Lynn
THE DOCTOR WHO MADE HER LOVE AGAIN	Susan Carlisle
THE MAVERICK WHO RULED HER HEART	Susan Carlisle
AFTER ONE FORBIDDEN NIGHT...	Amber McKenzie
DR PERFECT ON HER DOORSTEP	Lucy Clark